The Lost Prophets

 Published by Condor Industries P.O. Box 275 Derby, CT 06418.

FIRST EDITION.

ISBN-10: 0-9797783-0-1

ISBN-13: 978-0-9797783-0-8

Dedicated to Bill, Betty, and Bobby,

With our love and gratitude...

Foreward

He was the winner of the 1978 Nobel Prize in literature, for his works which depicted Jewish life in Poland before and during World War II. His books transported me to another world. A world foreign to my upbringing, but, at the same time, very similar. Probably because his stories asked eternal questions burning inside all of us: Why am I here? What does God want of me? Where is He? What becomes of me after death? Why is there evil in the world?

For the most part, the themes in his art depicted the fall and redemption of the human spirit, as tested by a people whose culture was displaced as they wandered throughout the world. A people whose faith was forged repeatedly by the injustices of prejudice, the atrocities committed by the Nazis highlighted their plight.

On this special day, he had given a speech and advice to the hundreds who were in attendance. His message on writing literature was simple – just like his novels. Know your religion, know your history, and keep abreast of current events and politics. Then he said, “Let the Eskimos write about the Eskimos, write about what you know.”

After his talk, I and three other students had the privilege to meet him for a private audience. Imagine my embarrassment when, one by one, the other students brought books for him to sign. I didn’t think to bring even one and I owned a copy of every single book he had ever written.

“He must think I’m a fool! A knucklehead! An idiot! Why didn’t I realize this was the reason I was here – to get his autograph! Why didn’t I bring a book for him to sign? How stupid of me – again!”

Isaac Bashevis Singer turned my way, and I felt the heat in my face as I blushed.

“Do you have a book?” He asked.

I couldn’t speak.

“Do you have a book?” He repeated, a little annoyed at my blank expression. His light blue eyes looked at me as if they saw deep into my soul. His old thin frame seemed tired – like it was out of its element and uncomfortable with all the attention it was getting. Irritated, his body longed to be home, maybe in bed.

"No Sir, I'm sorry," I said.

"Well, if that's the way you are going to be," he paused, "at least let me shake your hand." An impish smile appeared on his exhausted face, transforming it with adolescent like glee.

We shook hands…

The Lost Prophets is a simpleton's attempt to follow Mr. Singer's advice, and "Let the Eskimos write about the Eskimos…"

Gimpel Lee

Prologue

Throughout the year 1812, the British Empire was expanding; their Armada was a dominant force throughout the world, and they were at war with the United States. Since it proclaimed its independence from England in July of 1776, the young United States nation struggled to keep its union intact.

James Madison was President, and the bulk of the nation's navy was comprised of six small battleships – classified frigates – one of which, the USS *Constitution*, is still commissioned in today's Navy.

During this period, the United States had internal political conflicts between those in the west and those in the south who wanted war for territory expansion motives, and those against it, primarily in New England, citing fears it would put a stranglehold on the nation's already crippled shipping industry.

As such, President Madison had a difficult time funding the military, and desertion was commonplace. The war was lost, except for a miracle.

On August 19th, 1812, the USS *Constitution* engaged the British ship HMS *Guerriere*, off the coast of Nova Scotia, and won. The battle inspired the young nation that a victory against Great Britain was possible, and public sentiment turned to support the war.

During this battle, sailors witnessed British cannon balls bouncing off the USS *Constitution*, and that is how the ship acquired the nickname, "Old Ironsides." This legend is taught in grade school history books.

What is rarely known is that Isaac Hull, the Commodore of "Old Ironsides," hailed from a region in Connecticut called The Lower Naugatuck Valley. It is an area comprised of several towns: Shelton, Seymour, Beacon Falls, Ansonia, Naugatuck, Oxford and Derby. He was born in Derby.

A story from this old land, first settled by people of the Paugussett Nation, proclaims the oak installed on the side of the ship, during the famous battle, came from the Valley foothills. Hull routinely called on the river port town of Derby to perform maintenance to the battleship, in this once thriving city nicknamed "New Boston."

During a rush repair, it is said, the oak planking used was not thoroughly dried, and because of this, many believe the cannon balls fired from the *Guerriere* deflected off the *Constitution.* There are others who believe a supernatural force field was at work.

Throughout the Naugatuck Valley, in the taverns, barbershops and factories, arguments have been made for both sides that without this occurring, the battle might have been lost and the United States would have collapsed.

The maintenance work lasted four days, and the stay was not without intrigue. In fear of being caught by the British, Hull decided to secretly visit Derby instead of his usual ports in Rhode Island and New Hampshire.

Of course, once he moored the ship in Derby, it did not take long before British troops were alerted of the situation, and Hull narrowly escaped capture by sailing down river just one hour before British troops arrived.

Before he fled, it is said that his mother put a mysterious book, *The Book of Lost Prophets,* in his cabin. The manuscript was given to Isaac Hull's father, Joseph, by a dying Islamic holy man; who years earlier, he had hidden from certain death during one of his trade voyages to the West Indies.

Joseph Hull's providing refuge to the Islamic Holy man was unprecedented, as the Christian sailors of the west, were routinely ransacked, held hostage, or sold into slavery by the Muslim pirates who controlled the Barbary Coast of the Mediterranean Sea.

It is important to note, in 1797 the historic Treaty of Tripoli, which addressed the piracy, was written in Arabic and negotiated aboard the USS *Constitution*.

A few years after inheriting *The Book of Lost Prophets*, Joseph Hull, and a group of Derbyites, had captured a British ship that was bombarding the coastal town of Stratford, Connecticut.

Hidden under canvas, except for Hull, who in order to deceive an enemy Sentry pretended to be drunk: they sailed down the Housatonic River at night, surprised the British ship, and saved the neighboring city from destruction.

To the applause from townspeople on the banks of the river, the captured ship was sailed back to the Derby "Narrows" shipyards as a trophy. It was on this ship that young Isaac Hull learned to sail.

Stories circulated that, until the 1970's, *The Book of Lost Prophets* was passed along to certain people of the area, this included individuals from all religious denominations. During its stay, The Valley prospered from the age of the maritime, to the Industrial Revolution.

Of note, The Valley can lay claim to the Howe Pin machine. This invention, by Dr. John Howe, enabled the mass production of the "common pin," and hence made the concept of mass production feasible which ignited the Industrial Revolution.

For over 150 years, thousands of Valley people, from diverse ethnic and religious upbringings, peacefully worked together in factories pumping out pins, which fed the garment industry. In the late 1970's, the last pin manufacturing company, The Star Pin, went out of business.

The Book of Lost Prophets is believed to have been destroyed. But it is the hope of many who know its value and power, that this holy book is only misplaced.

Article 11 of The Treaty of Peace and Friendship, known as the Treaty of Tripoli:

"As the Government of the United States of America is not, in any sense, founded on the Christian religion; as it has in itself no character of enmity against laws, religion, or tranquility, of Mussulmen, and, as the said States never entered into any war, or act of hostility against any Mahometan nation, it is declared by the parties, that no pretext arising from religious opinions, shall ever produce an interruption of the harmony existing between the two countries."

The Treaty of Tripoli was ratified in 1797 by unanimous vote on the Senate floor during John Adams' Presidency.

Chapter 1

"Life and death are void of ambiguities when nourished by truth." Translated from The Book of Lost Prophets, *Circa 200 A.D.*

It was April 5, 1975. The Steelers had won the Super Bowl, Bobby Fisher refused to play Anatoly Karpov in chess, *Baretta* and *Welcome Back Kotter* were premiering on television, while the heyday of *The Odd Couple* and *Gunsmoke* was over. Pope Paul VI was the Cardinal of Rome, and a war in the country of Vietnam was about to officially end. Ryan Walsh would graduate from high school in June, and he had so hoped that his dad could attend; but his father didn't make it, he died.

Near the time of his father's death, this particular Saturday morning, Ryan bent down to kiss his forehead. His father's blue eyes stared up at him, and his chapped lips beckoned Ryan to come closer.

"Soon we all…" There was a short pause as his father summoned his final words, "must say enough." It was evident to Ryan "enough" came out louder than the other words, but Ryan wasn't sure what his father meant.

Ryan sat on the bed and lit him an Old Gold cigarette. Aunt Mary had just tended to his father by changing the bed sheets, and putting new pajama bottoms on him. Ryan put the cigarette in his mouth, but his dad, Bill, couldn't inhale. He had no strength left. Ryan took a long drag, then breathed the smoke into his father's mouth, hoping his dying breath could siphon whatever nicotine it could. Aunt Mary came out from the bathroom and held Ryan's hand as they knelt to say the Rosary. His father died peacefully.

Ryan noticed his eyes widen and look at him as if to say, "Don't worry, everything will be alright." Then the death rattle in his throat stopped. The little croup-like sound you could hear every time he breathed for the last three days, ended.

Aunt Mary had told him, "When you hear that sound, death will not be long."

Ryan wasn't sure what he had meant by, "Soon we all must say enough," so now he figured his father was talking about the acceptance of death. But he wasn't one-hundred percent certain and that was because his father had always talked in riddles and parables and Ryan had often misunderstood what he meant.

To Ryan, his father's life was typical, if not mundane. Because his father had died young, Bill Walsh was raised by his mother. He went to the local Derby High School, got a job at the Star Pin factory, where his father, Ryan's grandfather, was once the General Manager, and married his wife Catherine, who bore him a child – Ryan. She too died and left Bill a widower. He never remarried and he raised his son alone.

He was not rich, and never traveled to far off places. He never held political office and he never participated in athletics. He never went to fancy restaurants. He never had an expensive car and he never cussed or spoke ill of anyone.

He lived in a five-room apartment and rarely missed a day of work. He loved people, cigarettes, beer, reading, and listening to Herb Alpert.

Yet, as Ryan watched the undertakers remove his father's corpse from the bed, with the realization came a tremendous void that befell not just himself, but everyone. Bill was a respected elder in the community, and Ryan had regrets.

Lately he found himself agitated with every word his father spoke and any meaning his stoic life represented. And Ryan had let his feelings spill over to insults and arguments about God and their inherited faith.

"The Catholic Church is corrupt! Didn't they sell indulgences to get to Heaven?" Ryan argued.

His father would agree, which only served to incite Ryan with more intense anger.

"Then how can you be a Catholic? Are you a fool?"

His father would never raise his voice.

"Who am I to question God's will? I can only be obedient to what is revealed to me, Ryan."

Bill would drink his coffee and take a puff from his cigarette as he calmly listened to his son's objections.

Ryan's face would turn red from frustration.

"All these books you read are an escape from reality. How can you know the real world if you never read modern works?" Ryan complained referring to the various religious books his father poured through each night after work.

For Ryan, Vonnegut, Salinger, Pynchon and Joyce were the authors of choice. One day his father, in an attempt to understand Ryan's reasoning, took Joyce's, *Finnegan's Wake*, with him to read in bed. The next night, Ryan inquired how he liked the book.

"Ryan, I am not an educated man. I'm sorry, but I did not understand what he was trying to say. It made no sense to me."

Ryan shook his head and said in a disgusted tone, "Dad, you are so unsophisticated!"

His father was not formally educated past high school, but he would not read a book without a dictionary next to him. So, he took as a compliment, what Ryan meant as an insult.

"Thank you, Ryan."

Ryan stormed out of the kitchen and went to his bedroom. He couldn't understand why his father wasn't insulted. To Ryan, this just proved his father was a fool or a simpleton, and Ryan felt embarrassed for him. Finally though, Ryan decided to get a dictionary and show his dad what the word "sophisticated" actually meant.

To Ryan's astonishment: he read: v. so.phis.ti.cat.ed: 1: to alter deceptively. 2: to deprive of genuineness, naturalness or simplicity. 3: to make complicated or complex.

At that moment, a truth was revealed to Ryan. His father was not sophisticated, or a simpleton; he just lived a simple life.

In June, Ryan Walsh graduated from high school, sold his home, and went to college. He never wanted to go back to Derby. He had regrets. Besides, the truth was his father was dead, and Ryan had said "enough."

Enough to living in a blue-collar town and to playing the part of a human guinea pig, breathing in countless carcinogens from soot stained brick factories. Enough to dressing the role of the thankless working class victim, toiling each week for small wages. Enough to being around small-minded people, who weren't worldly and educated enough to form progressive decisions. Enough to daily worshipping a God who never responded, and was used as a concoction, mixed with dogma and fear, to suppress man's drive.

Ryan Walsh was leaving Derby, and he missed his father. He had regrets. But now he struggled with what his father had meant when he said, "Soon we all must say enough."

Ryan was haunted by those six words. What did his father mean? Would he ever find out? How could he reconcile any guilt, or show any love, to a person who was dead? Was there a way to do so?

Ryan suppressed these questions, and functioned with the bouts of anxiety and depression they produced, until one week, like a cancer out of remission, they erupted and haunted every other thought he had.

"'Soon we all must say enough.' What did he mean?"

Chapter 2

"One wise man warned him not to look back while another shouted, 'turn and view all that your life's path hath trampled." Translated from The Book of Lost Prophets, *Circa 100 B.C.*

Ryan Walsh played golf regularly in North Scottsdale and for the past several years had attended every single Final Four, Super Bowl and World Series. Three times, during this run, he flew to Augusta and attended the Masters. Ryan owned a gorgeous house on Lake Shore Drive in Bay Village, Ohio, bordering Lake Erie. He had a yearly salary of $330,000 and an almost unlimited expense account.

He traveled the world, and met with such dignitaries as: President Ronald Reagan – Ryan contributed to the Republican Party, Pope John Paul II – Ryan's friend from Iceland is a member of the Knights of Malta, and Princess Diana – he had attended a fundraiser for Third World Orphans. One July night in Paris, Ryan was privileged to have danced with the Princess. She passed away shortly after.

By all accounts, Ryan was a likable person with a self-effacing manner. Handsome, with high cheekbones, thick brown hair, and light blue eyes: in business, he was able to ingratiate his clients by poking fun at himself. In particular, he had a slight stutter that he used to his advantage and it was humor instead of aggravation that surfaced when people finished his words.

When they did finish his words, he always laughed and said something along the lines of, "Whew, thank you," or "Easy for you to say." When he stammered and no one finished his sentence, Ryan always winked. This was to acknowledge his listener's patience, and the fact that he had just stuttered.

Everyone enjoyed Ryan Walsh's company. Everyone, that is, except for Ryan Walsh.

This cold December morning Ryan had to dress, and attend a meeting at his boss's office building on Ninth Street in downtown Cleveland. His employment depended on it, and this meant that the life Ryan had come to know demanded it. He wasn't queasy about the prospects of losing his livelihood, but he knew there was a problem. Lately Ryan felt numb.

Last night, after he had finished responding to emails, and half-heartedly planned his next days "To do" list, Ryan, as had become habit, poured himself a Scotch and contemplated his life. For years, this practice had no ill affect. He did his work proficiently and each day came and went as expected, that is until lately.

Now Ryan was on that proverbial "losing streak." For the last year, Ryan failed in his assignments, and it was apparent he had lost his business "edge." Ryan was told in no uncertain terms by his boss and friend, Tony Scarpa, that his next assignment would be his last if he did not succeed.

That was after he botched a deal, which would have brought NFL football to San Antonio. For some reason, Ryan, after spending the night entertaining influential decision makers, while bar hopping along the River Walk, he had called one of the city counsel members "Poncho," and another "Hop Sing." The men were insulted by Ryan's ethnic insensitivity, and voted against consummating a deal that should have been a slam dunk. That was the first time in his life Ryan had ever used such hurtful language to anyone. But it went downhill from there.

He worked for a public rep firm called Eskinsyness, Inc. The firm was comprised of a few lawyers and several salesmen like himself. Each was successful, and each drank, many times to excess. As is often the case in sales, drinking is never mentioned so long as you produce, but the minute you stop bringing in winning results, whispers among your peers circulate about alcohol affecting your work.

When an opening in the agency occurred, which had first brought Ryan to Eskinsyness; it was Mario Balducci who was the subject and target of such gossip. This time Ryan's drinking was being called into question, and Ryan knew that the only way to quell the inquest was to close a sales deal and prove he was not burnt out.

A part of Ryan, the numb part, was not scared about moving on in life and actually welcomed a change if he should lose his job. The other part of Ryan was afraid of losing all the perks, which his affluent livelihood afforded him.

Life, for Ryan, was not very difficult. If he soiled a suit, he just purchased another. If he damaged his car, he bought another. It was evident, in his mind, that most women loved money. So, when the need arose for sex, Ryan had plenty of phone numbers to call. All he had to do was decide the size, shape, and color. Lately Ryan hadn't made many phone calls to lady friends.

Last night he took a sip of Walker, and suddenly felt cold. Ryan didn't like the vibes among the others within his organization. The body language, and the conversations he heard, suggested he was the odd man out. Each guy in the agency, and there were ten, all got along amicably.

To Ryan, it was as if they were members of a "good ole boys club," and each always had the others' back. Ryan was an only child growing up, so the connection he felt to the other guys in the organization was important. It was all he had that mattered; and losing honor with them was humiliating.

Ryan unintentionally kicked a copy of *The Da Vinci Code*, before he bent down, picked it up, and placed it on the mahogany coffee table on the way to his master bedroom.

Ryan read certain books and he hoped to find inspiration in this one; but he was only entertained. He read the novel looking for something else.

"How did I get into this situation?" He mumbled to himself.

Ryan knew the answer to his complaint, but he diverted himself from even saying it, by concentrating on reading *The Da Vinci Code*. "How could there be such controversy about a work of fiction?" He wondered. He could not comprehend the heated debates concerning the upcoming movie, and he compared the dispute to the controversy over Oliver Stone's JFK movie. He especially found it hilarious when the conspiracy theorists talked about Da Vinci's masterpiece, *The Last Supper*. "It was painted 1,500 years after Christ's death," he thought. "It's not a Polaroid. Da Vinci was not there. How would Da Vinci know who was where at supper? How would he know where Mary Magdalene was sitting at all times? What's the big deal anyway?"

Ryan nodded his head, turned off his new Plasma TV, which was left on all night while he slept, and said the word, "Alcohol."

Although alcohol was the bullet that wounded his life, and put Ryan into his current dilemma, he knew the trigger was altogether different. No. To him it was not some evil gene lurking in his DNA that was masterminding the revolt of his mental makeup. To Ryan it was a simple choice. He liked to drink, but he couldn't deny the effect his consumptive habits had on his life. Lately he was haunted by his past.

It seemed he heard the voice of his father every second of every day. He couldn't think about the present without reliving his past, and he didn't know if it was the alcohol or just a more keen understanding of the connections in life.

Ryan brushed his teeth.

* * *

His ex-wife Deidre and he couldn't have children, and they never embraced each other like soul mates. She was a highly paid lawyer, and he was a successful Manufacturers' Rep. in the safety industry. Ryan's late aunt, Mary Beach, would most likely say they were not "blessed" with children. In any case, he figured, they attempted to be "blessed" for a few years. They tried fertility steroids, different foods, counseling, etc.

Finally, they gave up trying, and only concentrated on their careers. As ambition drove them both, Ryan and Deidre made a good deal of money, and had all the toys that wealth affords: a Benz for Deidre, and a Porsche for him, a golf membership at Fairfield, and a thirty-five foot twin engine yacht called *HaHa*, docked in Southport, Connecticut.

* * *

"I was too busy," he said, and then turned toward the medicine cabinet. He reached for his Polo Sport and dropped the bottle, shattering it on the Tuscan tiled floor. "Damn!" He shouted.

But his curse of the dropped bottle didn't deter his thoughts about his life with Deidre.

* * *

Ryan and Deidre purchased a house, which overlooked Long Island Sound. It had four bedrooms and five full baths, it was cedar sided and stained a Cape Cod gray, with a wrap around deck and a balcony coming off each bedroom. Ryan recalled the Saturday morning they purchased a ten-person hot tub, because that night they were hosting a party for a world-renowned rock band, that was practicing for an upcoming tour.

The band was living in Washington, a small hamlet in Northwestern Connecticut, but they visited Studio 54 in Manhattan and met friends of theirs, Nancy and Tom.

Nancy and Tom were "players" and partied with the band members. Somehow, everyone ended up invited to Ryan's house, and the hot tub was used all night. So were the four bedrooms. Nancy took each member on private tours of their home, while Deidre and Ryan talked politics and snorted coke in the tub. The band members found plenty of satisfaction that September evening.

* * *

Barefooted, Ryan danced backward to avoid stepping on the glass; then he walked to the closet and grabbed a broom and dustpan. He exhaled, swept up the glass, placed the shards into the wastebasket, and used a towel to wipe up the cologne. He reached for another bottle of Polo and slapped it on his face. Stepping forward, he grimaced. He had missed a piece of glass and it cut into his right foot.

"Shit!"

Ryan sat on the toilet and squeezed his foot, but he couldn't dislodge the shaving. Blood oozed from the entry, but the glass was not visible to him. After several minutes, he gave up trying to find it and washed his foot. Standing, Ryan felt pain, but it was not bad enough to spend more time paying it attention.

Ryan resumed his daydream.

* * *

His and Deidre's house was located in Westport, Connecticut. At that time, like the present, the town was one of the wealthiest cities, in one of wealthiest states, in one of the wealthiest nations, in the world. So you would figure life should not have been that difficult, but it was.

Ryan thought about the irony that they found themselves bored with the nights out on the town, and the parties with business partners, and high profile defense attorneys. They had strived for these associations, but grew restless once they reached this inner circle.

As was the case, Deidre came home one day and said, "Ryan, I want to try something new. I want to have an open marriage. I want to expand our love."

Ryan was receptive to anything that might stimulate their now floundering relationship and he listened. Deidre, being a great lawyer, gave a dissertation about their circumstances, like she was addressing a jury. She spoke with passion about fulfillment, love and honesty. Her reasoning had Ryan confused. To him her proposal was convoluted, but he didn't have to think about offering a counter opinion.

He figured. "When the football game is about to be lost, you throw up a 'Hail Mary' pass."

And so they tried an alternative lifestyle.

Ryan had his girlfriends and Deidre had her boyfriends and some young girlfriends too. They went to swingers' parties and committed every form of adultery one can imagine. For a while it worked. Different was fun. Different was exciting. Ryan would be in one bedroom with a woman, hearing Deidre moan in the other with another man. The liaisons became a game. Ryan had sex with two women one night, only to see Deidre arrive home with three men the next. Deidre was very competitive indeed.

* * *

Ryan reached into his downstairs closet, pulled out his blazer, and then put it on, when thoughts of his father once more haunted his brain.

* * *

He imagined what his father would have said. Because his dad was a mystic of sorts, Bill Walsh read books like, *Saint John of the Cross*, and often told Ryan about "The dark night of the soul." In fact, his father read every kind of existential and theology book he could get his hands on, books like: *The Letters of Saint Augustine*, as well as the works of philosophers like Socrates, Descartes, and Spinoza.

Although Bill Walsh was a Catholic, he read the Jewish Kabbalah and he often studied The Tree of Life. From Keter, to Malchut, and back, Ryan's father sought his own spiritual destiny, and he saw meaning in everything around him. The person hauling the trash, the dog next door, the tree out front: they all had a design intended for a particular purpose to him. Everything was special.

Bill often spoke to Ryan about the overlap of all faiths, and in particular, he pointed out that Saint Teresa of Avila, one of the doctors of faith in the Catholic Church, was also part Jewish. He explained to Ryan how she had laid the groundwork for Catholic mysticism, and how such concentrations were a gift from God.

So, practicing the doctrine of the ascetic, his father always made it a special point to warn Ryan about the sins of the flesh. He professed that people using each other in an unholy manner, only led to each hating one another. Ryan was young, but he listened to every word. He remembered it all, and he wanted to believe, but he couldn't muster the dedication required to try.

* * *

Ryan turned on the ignition to his Seville with the remote starter on his key chain. It was parked in the driveway, not in the garage where he thought it was. This way the car would be warmed up for the forty-minute ride to downtown Cleveland.

* * *

Right now, it dawned on Ryan, that his father's prophesy about sexually promiscuous behavior had come true. He recalled Deidre and his gradual marital break-up during the months of folly that they enjoyed. First, they degraded each other in bed like dogs, then they stopped being intimate, next they quit talking. Finally, they couldn't stomach looking at each other, and then they divorced.

* * *

Ryan got into his car, and drove toward the gate. Pressing the button located above the driver's side visor, the gate opened, and he turned right and headed to the interstate. He drove to his meeting with Tony Scarpa, but his thoughts were still on his father and ex-wife.

* * *

Three years ago Ryan happened to meet one of Deidre's old work cohorts in Boston. Smiling, the man, Jack Ell, informed Ryan of how Deidre had seduced a young man half her age that she had worked with in Stamford. The young man had a wife and two children, a girl of five and a boy of seven who had special needs. The wife found them in bed one afternoon at the young man's home. The couple divorced and the man's life shattered like fine china against a slate floor. They tried to reconcile, but couldn't.

The young wife eventually got on with her life and remarried, but the young man never recovered from the divorce. He went to a psychologist, highly recommended by Deidre, after his children no longer wanted to see him, but the visits were to no avail.

Months later, the young man checked into a hotel, that he and Deidre frequented, and shot a bullet into his head. After this, Deidre began to drink heavily. Her weight ballooned by fifty pounds, and she later suffered a nervous breakdown. Eventually, Deidre lost her job and moved back home to live with her mother in the town of Greenwich.

* * *

Ryan gripped the steering wheel tighter as he made the turn onto the highway; the final words that Jack Ell spoke resonated in his head.

"Hey, God served her right."

* * *

Ryan, although divorced ten years from Deidre, remembered not the Deidre of today, but the young, smiling beauty he had married, and somehow he felt responsible for her demise.

Yes. It was Deidre who wanted an open marriage, which eventually led to their divorce. But Ryan knew, in his gut, it was the wrong thing to do and he knew that from his father's teachings and actions.

"If I had just said no to her," he thought, "then maybe none of that would have happened?"

Ryan felt responsible for Deidre's fate, and he felt guilty for the young man's death, too. Mostly, Ryan worried that maybe Jack Ell could be correct. "If God served her right, what did He have in store for me?"

* * *

Finally, Ryan was able to break free of his past and the business side of him took control. The part of him that wanted to keep his high paying job, and all the perks, thought about his meeting with Tony Scarpa at Eskinsyness.

Tony and Ryan had been friends for close to thirty years. They were fraternity brothers in college when Ryan was a freshman. Tony was, in some ways, a business mentor to Ryan.

Ryan had worked for Tony, who was three years older, selling airfreight when he graduated from Dartmouth; Tony taught Ryan sales. Like how to ask probing questions, and how to ask for a sales order. Tony was a great sales person, and so was each member of the agency. Every one of them was fun to be around in a social setting.

Ryan pulled off the interstate to buy a coffee at a Dunkin Donuts. He thought about the time he had with Paul, the West Coast Rep., in Vegas last month. They had crashed a reunion for a Canadian Medical School, and pretended to be doctors by putting fake identification tags on their coats.

Ryan smiled as he paid the drive-thru lady for the medium coffee. The pretty Ecuadorian woman, about thirty, thought Ryan was smiling at her, and she returned the change with a wink. Ryan politely winked back, took the change, and then laughed as he drove out of the parking lot thinking about his Vegas trip.

It was times like the one in Vegas, with the other sales guys, that he cherished. That night Paul had grabbed the microphone on the stage, gave an impromptu speech to all in attendance, and then received a standing ovation from his fake "classmates."

Ryan loved that part of his profession, the zany and carefree attitude, which the guys in the agency exemplified. To him, Eskinsyness was more than just another lobbying group for the wealthy. It was a fraternity of salesmen, and it was a way of life. Pressed for an explanation of his job, he would always describe it rather than just say he worked for a "Rep firm."

Once Ryan explained it to a female acquaintance that he met at a bar, "Patty, most old money people lack the time or desire to hobnob with everyday business people. That's where guys like me come in. When money is on the line, and the grease needs to be applied to the wheels, guys like me are called. We get paid a handsome fee to bring the sale home, too. Let me put it another way, Patty," Ryan said as he stirred his drink and looked into her brown eyes.

"Do you remember those old Western movies, when there is a dispute over the rights to a waterhole, and the wealthy rancher hires a gunslinger to tilt ownership his way?"

Patty stared into his lips in a daze. This was a trained method. A technique that she employed to give the impression of her undivided attention.

"Well, we are the gunslingers of today," Ryan said. "We don't use muscle, or threats, or guns; we use Eskinsyness and money. A lot of money."

* * *

After parking his car in the lot, Ryan got out, took the ticket from the attendant, and walked across the street. His foot flared with pain from the embedded glass, and he instinctively shifted his body weight to his left side.

After exchanging "Good mornings," with Gus, the security guard, Ryan entered the elevator and pressed the 10th floor button for Eskinsyness, Inc. He opened the large oak door to the office and was greeted by Janet, Tony's assistant.

"Good morning, Ryan. How was your weekend?"

"Just great, Janet. I trust yours went well," he said, and then sat on the couch next to Tony's door.

Waiting for Tony, Ryan inspected his clothing to make sure everything was in place. He had on a blue blazer, a one-hundred per cent cotton, blue striped button down shirt, pleated Khaki pants that were cuffed, and brown Johnson & Murphy shoes. He always tried to blend in, and was a complete opposite from Tony, who always dressed up, and tried to carry the room.

Tony spent four thousand dollars each, for fine Italian made suits. Armani and Brioni were the only styles he wore. Tony would always joke that Eskinsyness was a suit factory in Italy. Ryan never knew whether or not Tony was kidding, because it was Tony's agency and he had named it Eskinsyness. Fondly referred to as "Bull Shit, Inc." by business associates.

At nine o'clock Tony opened his door, and waved Ryan into his office. Shaking Tony's hand, Ryan noticed the gold chain that he had around his wrist was new, and his shoes appeared to be recently purchased as well. Ryan sat in the black leather chair in front of Tony's oversized tiger oak desk, which had been given to him when his father passed, and he waited for Tony to speak.

Tony had large brown eyes and drooping flesh on both his eyelids and underneath the sockets; the loose flesh actually shook when he bobbed his head. But features like these, which might usually be considered repulsive, commanded respect on the face of Tony, much like a war wound did on a veteran military soldier.

He was a confident person, and his belief in himself, generated the esteem of his associates and everyone he dealt with, from clients, to his barber, to his bartender. The sagging bags of flesh on his eyes oozed with a certain leadership quality that spoke volumes to his work ethic.

"Ryan, I won't keep you long. You know what's at stake here for both of us."

Ryan was happy Tony was not pulling any punches. Tony had a tendency to belabor a point, and Ryan was hoping not to get a lecture about his job performance. Many meetings with Tony went off on a tangent, and Ryan had to sit up and listen in a total submissive posture, while Tony's voice spewed forth the newest jargon in business talk. Words like, Synergistically, or buzz phrases like, "At the end of the day," always found their way into a sentence.

Tony put a computer memory disc in front of Ryan.

"We have a lucrative deal in the works for a trash to energy plant, but we need the vote from an alderman, and we need the property rights of a local bar," Tony said.

Ryan was relieved. The company was probably TR Industries and Ryan helped secure two other sites for them three years ago. This, he figured, would be an easy task. In Ryan's mind, Tony was throwing him a softball to hit, and after performing this, his job would not be in question. His lifestyle would remain in tact.

"Thanks, Tony," Ryan said, and picked up the disc. "Where's the job?"

"Ryan, that's the good part," Tony grinned while putting his suit coat on a hanger and adjusting his silk suspenders, "Derby, Connecticut. Your childhood city."

He knew Ryan had a problem with his hometown, from the way he always avoided talking about his youth, but he had never learned exactly what the issue was. Tony just knew Ryan clammed up whenever he was asked where he was from, and this was Tony's way of giving Ryan a free pass, but it was also a way to put Ryan's nose in crap. That way, Tony could justify, in his mind, the sales gift he had just given him.

Ryan nodded his head, took the disc, and went toward the door before turning back and saying, "Thanks again, I appreciate it, Tony."

"It's not what you think Ryan. This is a very important job for the agency, and I know you have connections there. Everything should be on file, if not, just call."

Ryan walked out, and immediately thought about his life in Derby. It was a past he had not visited in over thirty years.

Chapter 3

"If you betray your neighbor, you betray yourself and you betray Allah." Translated from The Book of Lost Prophets*, Circa 400 A.D.*

Sharma and Jack Zawadski moved to Derby, Connecticut from Union, New Jersey in 1992. They purchased an old tavern downtown. Sharma ran the business, while Jack worked for a liquor distributor seven miles away in New Haven.

They were active in the community and although Jack and Sharma had no children of their own, they volunteered in the local youth sports programs. Jack helped out with the Pop Warner football team, while Sharma coached softball and raised money to fund the city's first hockey organization. It was named the Ralph Gallo Hockey League, after her late father, and Sharma coached the Rangers.

Derby was settled in 1675 and Sharma affectionately nicknamed the area, "The land that time forgot." Indeed, their bar was established in 1786; and, except for updates to the kitchen, it maintained most of the original bar, woodwork, and floorboards. At first, the residents of the Valley reminded her of a throw back to older times, too.

For instance, years ago, hundreds rallied to rebuild a house for a young couple and they did it in four days. What made the act newsworthy by CNN was that the couple had mistakenly let their insurance lapse by ten days and coverage had been dropped by their insurer. Since it was just prior to the Christmas Holidays, the CNN piece portrayed the insurance company's spokesman as the heartless Mr. Potter from the old movie classic, *It's A Wonderful Life*. He was a pudgy man of about sixty, with a round face and loose jowls that gave him the appearance of an English Bull Dog.

The citizens of Derby were juxtaposed with clips of the film; and, if viewed mid-way, it seemed like an advertisement for a remake of the movie. The exclamation point to this was when they showed the Police Chief, who resembled the actor Jimmy Stewart from the movie classic – thin, boyish looks – on a ladder replacing a window in the house. The title for the expose was, “The Valley of Brotherly Love.”

That’s why Sharma and Jack were devastated, six months previous, when news that the town officials wanted to invoke the right to imminent domain and build a trash to energy plant on property called O’Sullivan’s Island, to which their Brass Monkey tavern was needed for truck access. How could they do this to them? What would Sharma and Jack do? Didn’t they have a conscience? Were there not scruples to be considered?

Sharma, in particular, felt betrayed. Most of the citizens, from polls taken by the town’s newspaper, *The Evening Sentinel*, wanted the plant constructed. The ten-year tax assessment had just been completed, and everyone was paying higher taxes. Derby, being the smallest city in Connecticut, was landlocked and had difficulty expanding its revenue base. So, the trash plant promised to alleviate some of the tax burden.

A group of citizens opposed the plant and Sharma naturally gravitated to them. Meetings were held at each other’s houses and one lady in particular, Antonella DeLucia, and Sharma talked often; the two of them soon became best friends.

* * *

On this Tuesday, Sharma stopped by Antonella’s home for a visit. They were two women in the prime of their lives, who both found comfort in their new friendship.

"Sharma, would you like some tea?"

"Hell no. I'll take some coffee Nell." Sharma answered, then turned around to look at the different religious pictures Antonella had in one corner of the living room. Sharma never mentioned them, but she found the keepsakes comforting. *The Black Madonna*, holding the black baby Jesus, in particular, reminded Sharma of her Polish grandmother who resided on Kennedy Boulevard in Jersey City. Her father was half Polish and from him Sharma inherited her light blonde hair.

A car honked, and Sharma looked out the second floor apartment window. She noticed a taxi in front of the house across the street. It was a new taxi and new to Derby, too. Sharma was not a stupid person and she understood what the taxi represented. As the older residents passed on, people were moving into the affordable Derby apartments from bigger cities like Bridgeport, Norwalk, and New York.

Most of these newcomers couldn't afford cars and they spent money on transportation just to get to the supermarket. Sharma learned that some spared the expense of a taxi or bus by calling 911 and faking a sickness, to be rushed to the hospital by an ambulance, only to got off the stretcher and walk down the street to the mall. To Sharma, these people were shameless con artists and gypsies.

Sharma figured that someone like Antonella could not possibly grasp what this meant, but Sharma could and it was troubling to her. She had moved to Derby for the tranquility. She settled here, as a young bride, to be around people like Nell. She left Jersey for Derby, in part, to escape the people who were now moving in.

She wouldn't get into a discussion with Nell about the taxi's significance or even about the recently opened pawnshop on Main Street, because she didn't want to scare her. To Sharma, the pawnshop represented a drug addict's bank. A place where crazed scoundrels could barter to raise money for drugs or bail. Objects, which were probably stolen, would be given a cash value and the money handed over to the dealer or bail bondsman, so they could be freed, or get high, or both.

Besides, she also thought that Antonella would brush off her concerns as if they were of no worry. There were certain things, in the ways of the world that Sharma couldn't explain to Antonella, because she considered her a little naïve.

* * *

"It's past five, how bout some Buca?" Antonella asked with a crooked smile that was appealing to men and women alike.

"Sure Nell, why not?"

"Sharma, black or white Sambuca?"

"For Crissake Nell, I feel like I'm at the Monkey,'" she said. Then, licking her full lips, she slowly pronounced her choice, "Black."

Antonella laughed, and poured the alcohol into the espresso coffee cup.

For the next hour, they talked about the proposed trash plant. Sharma hated the idea of losing her business and shook her head as she complained to Antonella.

"Bastards!" She said, and banged her right hand on the kitchen table, rattling the tiny espresso cup resting in the saucer.

Antonella reached out and took her hand. Her hand was soft, but firm, and the gesture made Sharma feel right. It also made her believe she had befriended a soul who was out of step with the world she was born into. A world Sharma viewed as cut throat. Regardless, Antonella and the group she organized, called P.R.I.D.E., was all Sharma had to fight for her business.

* * *

The sun shone through the kitchen window and onto Sharma's tanned face and blonde hair. Antonella could see her roots were still intact, and showed no signs of aging – unnatural for a woman pushing forty. It was obvious to Antonella, that Sharma visited a tanning booth, because around her eyes were telltale white rings: obviously from the protective glasses she had to wear.

Antonella knew, as she comforted Sharma and told her that P.R.I.D.E. would prevail, that Sharma did not believe her. But it didn't matter to Antonella. In her mind, Sharma would understand when the trash to energy plant was voted down and turned away.

Antonella liked what she saw in Sharma's heart, but she also detected there was a lot of hurt in her, too. Antonella believed that the rough exterior, which Sharma exuded, was a defense mechanism that guarded the pain within her. It was something Sharma didn't want to discuss.

"Sharma are you going to the Alderman's meeting Thursday night with me?"

"Absolutely Nell. Us against them Bastards, right?" Then she laughed, holding her right hand against her forehead.

* * *

Sharma had to go to the meetings, but she found them boring. Members of the P.R.I.D.E. group would take turns at the podium reciting various reasons why the plant should not be developed, and Sharma couldn't determine whether the group was actually making an impact. She found the group's sincerity embarrassing next to the underlying agenda of the politicians, which was money and votes.

She believed there was probably graft involved, but she couldn't discuss this with Antonella. One time, when Sharma hinted that Mayor McHugh was on the take, Antonella actually scolded her.

"That can't be. He is only thinking about what is good for the city, it's just a bad decision." Antonella had said.

Sharma knew a victory was a long shot, but it was the only shot she had. In her head, she had already conceded defeat, but she hoped that the money to be offered for her business would at least be fair market value.

Sharma sipped her espresso, looked at the relaxed expression on Antonella's face, and felt shameful.

Yesterday Sharma had a phone conversation with Mayor McHugh, of which she didn't want Antonella to know. It was about the buyout. The Mayor had told her that a man was arriving from Cleveland to address the matter. And the man was going to make her husband an offer for their property. Until she met with the company's representative from Ohio, Sharma would continue to support P.R.I.D.E., but she sensed that her days of assisting the group would end very soon.

* * *

Antonella sat across the table and looked at Sharma's glistening hair, brown eyes, and athletic build. Her appearance fit that of a professional tennis player, and her edgy temperament to win made Antonella imagine that Sharma would have been a champion if in that arena.

But she knew Sharma did not like going to the meetings. She could tell by the way one side of her face drooped whenever people got up to speak against the plant; it was evident to Antonella that Sharma didn't care to win this fight.

She knew Sharma had an unfavorable opinion toward the poorer people moving into the town from the larger cities, too. Their hair was different, their skin was different, they smelled different, they talked different; but Antonella also knew they were no different than how Sharma's and her grandparents were when they arrived to America a century ago.

Antonella grasped the nature of the situation. She sensed that some of the newcomers were scared moving into the new surroundings, and they carried themselves with a look of indignation as they went about town- many defiantly walked in the streets. But she also believed, if Sharma and the new residents gave each other a chance, everyone would win out.

Antonella was of the opinion that Sharma didn't want to sell her business, but that she probably would for the right price. Antonella was also informed that a representative from the trash plant was visiting to present Sharma and Jack with an offer, but she wouldn't hold it against Sharma if she did sell out.

In Antonella's heart, Sharma didn't understand that to sell her property was not in her or her neighbor's ultimate best interest. If she did so, where would she go, to the suburbs?

What would be gained by that? Weren't there neighbors in the suburbs, too?

She remembered her mother once said, "Antonella, a holy man told me, that there is a fine line between running from something, and running to something."

But, because Antonella figured Sharma was a little naïve in the ways of the universe, she would never hold it against her if she did sell her property.

There were certain things Antonella couldn't explain to Sharma because she didn't want to alarm her. Antonella just figured Sharma knew the right answers inside her soul, and wouldn't betray the truth, once she faced it.

Antonella believed the Almighty lived inside everyone, and to betray your self, was to betray God.

Chapter 4

"Memories are the history of the eternal, distort and shroud them, but you never escape them. You can only embrace them – the good ones and the bad-for they make us complete." Translated from The Book of Lost Prophets, *Circa 25 A.D.*

It was December 14th, and, although the holidays were still over two weeks away, Newark International was busy with people traveling home. From businessmen like Ryan, to Tibetan priests, to an Up With People singing group, to young families on their way to vacation at Disney, to retirees and college students, the airport had that distinct holiday rush feeling, and

Ryan instinctively walked in rhythm with everyone else as he headed for the baggage claim area.

Ryan felt alone as he walked. Each of these people was enthusiastically traveling home to see loved ones they cared about. To visit relatives and friends they connected with, while Ryan had no one to visit. Ryan was going home for the first time in over thirty years, but it was not a joyous occasion.

For Ryan, there was no one to hug, or kiss, or to share a laugh with over dinner. For him there was no one to take his hand and lead him to something magical, like a surprise present, or a party, or a walk down a snow filled street.

To Ryan, there was only the learned social graces of doing business, and he knew that when he arrived in Derby, the experience would not likely be warm and fuzzy. How could it be a joyous homecoming when his heart had regrets?

Having worked Metro New York for years, Ryan was very familiar with the area; he felt comfortable walking down the airport concourse. He stopped, bought a pretzel, and looked out the window to the New York skyline off in the distance. Gone were the World Trade Centers and Ryan wondered if, on a clear day, the Empire State Building and the Chrysler Building were still visible over the Jersey City hillside.

The hillside included cities that bordered the west side of the Hudson River like Hoboken, West New York, Bayonne, Union

City, and others, of which the biggest was Jersey City. Manhattan bordered the east side of the river and ran parallel to that stretch of cities.

Ryan took a bite from his pretzel and thought about his assignment in Derby, and that triggered thoughts of his father.

* * *

Ryan never knew his mother since she had died in his first years of life, but his father made sure he knew how much she loved him. His dad never went into detail about her death; it was a subject too painful for him to recall, and Ryan knew better than to ask. But now, he wished that he had.

* * *

Ryan looked at a vendor selling 911 mementos. From hats, to shirts, to glasses and posters, the stand was dedicated to images of the trade centers or of the NYPD, and FDNY. Ryan was in no hurry like the other people, and he ate his pretzel.

* * *

"Remember Ryan," his father would often say with a Bible in his hand, "when all else fails, say a prayer for enlightenment." The Bible was not there for dramatic effect, but the book was there much like a wallet would be in any man's pocket. It was a necessary item.

Besides the Bible, their five-room apartment was a living-breathing library of religious readings. Thomas Kempis,

Thomas Merton, Saint Augustine, Saint Teresa of Avila, Cardinal Sheen, Saint Thomas Aquinas, and hundreds of others were on all the bookshelves. If Ryan came in to watch the television, the backside of *The Way of the Cross* or *The Interior Castle* made for good coasters. These books happened to be hardcover books, and milk or juice stain rings were easily wiped clean.

In the morning, when Ryan went into the bathroom to wash up, chances were good that a recently deceased person's Mass card would be wedged into the molding around the mirror. If he did not look down, Ryan would most certainly trip on a book like, *Confessions,* as it was very thick.

If a book fell off the coffee table, because they were stacked up like a leaning tower, novena cards would fall out. By his facial grimaces, Ryan knew his father got annoyed at this, because the novena cards doubled as bookmarkers. Why it should matter, Ryan didn't understand. Each of these books was read not just once, but hundreds of times. In the case of *No Man is an Island*, it was most likely read over one thousand times.

And so, it went for him with Bill Walsh. They were father and son living on the second floor of a three family house without the comfort and softness of a woman.

For the most part, there was always a serene peace at their home. Only when Uncle James came to visit, did it get loud. On those occasions, his father and uncle would drink beer after beer and discuss religion. Many topics were bridged in rapid succession between the two.

"Is the Pope infallible?" Uncle James would ask.

"Yes. In matters of faith and morals," his father responded.

"How do you know there is a God?"

"Through faith," his father replied without hesitation.

"What exactly is grace?" Uncle James would probe.

And so, it went for hours…

"Can a man redeem himself after he has engaged in deadly sins his whole life?"

"Saint Augustine was a terrible sinner and he repented." Ryan's father pointed out.

Ryan would sit in the living room and listen. When it was time for him to sleep, he would sneak out from under the covers, and watch the two brothers through the half closed door to his bedroom. As loud as they would get, on those occasions, they ended the night with a hug.

Without fail, Ryan watched as his father staggered into the other bedroom and knelt down to say his prayers. Kissing the Holy Scapular to Saint Anthony that hung around his neck, he would tumble into bed. The Scapular was a laminated picture of the saint on the front, and a prayer for strength to him on the back. An inexpensive brown cotton lanyard was attached to it, and went around his neck like a chain.

It was given to Bill, by his mother, when he was confirmed in the Holy Spirit at the age of thirteen, it was a reminder to stay humble and charitable, and pledge service to the child Jesus.

With such reminders around him, Ryan always felt safe. Even when he had to be left alone, while his father worked overtime, there was always a presence of security. In Ryan's mind, the Holy Spirit stood guard by the kitchen table, where the entrance door was located. The door was never locked. There was never a need to lock it.

* * *

Ryan swallowed the last piece of pretzel. He headed down the escalator to baggage claim area C, and saw an employee from Continental Airlines wearing Cofra Safety Shoes. When he had his safety business, Ryan sold them that brand. The shoes had composite safety toes, and did not set off the metal detectors every time an employee passed through a secured zone.

He retrieved his luggage, one black leather garment bag and a matching mid-size duffle, then followed the signs and walked by two National Guardsmen – one female – and to the shuttle. The shuttle was called the Air Train, and it took him to Penn Station in Newark. From there, the train transported him to Penn Station in Manhattan. Next, he would take a cab to Grand

Central, board Metro North to Bridgeport, Connecticut, then change trains and go ten miles north to Derby. Renting a car would have been faster and easier, but Ryan was in no hurry to arrive at his hometown.

When he got off the train in New York, he lugged his two bags up a flight of stairs, and was reminded of the glass, imbedded in his foot, when he pressed down to turn right on the top step. He waited at the corner of 31st and 8th Avenue, in rain, and hailed a cab to the Grand Central Station.

After he arrived at Grand Central and purchased his ticket to Derby, Ryan walked up the marble stairs to the second floor, and sat at the bar. He had time to spare and decided to get himself a drink or two. Looking down, he noticed that the horde of commuters was in constant motion, but not chaotic.

Everyone had traveled through the terminal so often, that it appeared every inch of space was used to its maximum level of efficiency. No one deviated from their routine paths. It seemed like every hesitation, every cutoff, and every sidestep was done like a routine dance.

Ryan tried to get the barkeep's attention by tapping his credit card on the granite counter, but he was busy talking to a customer and had been for too long. The bartender was a young man, and seemed to be soliciting a job interview from the customer. The customer, an older man in his forties, looked interested, but Ryan could tell he really didn't care. The man was being polite. Eventually, the bartender sensed the man's disinterest, and backed off. Finally, he noticed Ryan.

Ryan gave no indication that he was aggravated by the bartender's lackadaisical effort, and asked for a Johnnie Walker on the rocks.

He thanked the young guy for the drink, gave him a two-dollar tip, and then sat back.

He noticed that the same style safety vests he had sold the Transit Authority ten years ago were still being worn. The workers, who walked from the terminal through the Central Hall to another terminal, to check with Conductors, perform maintenance, and retrieve items found on the trains, all were wearing them –this made Ryan feel good, and kind of proud.

He remembered feeling that same way when his buddy Matt and he had worked with New York Fire developing a new flashlight, or the time he and two other friends, Eddie and Frank, were able to sell a new style delineator post to the Bridge and Tunnel Authority, after it passed a longevity test in the Brooklyn Battery Tunnel. Achievements like these helped people, saved lives, and made Ryan feel connected to New York. To him, it was his fingerprint on the city.

He took another sip of Scotch, and then admired the splendor of the terminal. The marble floors, oak trim, and hand painted celestial cathedral ceilings were in stark contrast to when he first saw the building as a youth.

Back then, the terminal was a mess and slated to become an office complex after its landmark status was pulled, but Jackie Onassis Kennedy spearheaded its renovation and rescued it. To Ryan, this was her fingerprint on New York. Ryan took another sip of Scotch and thought back to the first time he saw Grand Central Station.

* * *

He was about ten, and his Aunt Mary took him there for a day out in the city. Her four friends all had girls around his age, or younger, and she asked Ryan to accompany her, because all six of Aunt Mary's children were older.

They spent the day going to the Statue of Liberty by ferry, to the United Nations, Mama Leone's restaurant, and finally to the Match Game at the NBC studios.

* * *

Ryan ordered another drink.

* * *

He tried to remember if they had visited Saint Patrick's Cathedral, but he couldn't recall. That day, they arrived back at Grand Central cold and exhausted, having walked from Rockefeller Center on a late November day. Ryan imagined he could still feel the chill on his cheeks and nose, as if it had just happened today.

The terminal was a pigsty. Papers were strewn about; garbage cans were over filled, the paint on the ceiling was old and chipping, and, as if the dilapidation wasn't bad enough, the whole place smelled like urine. Some people slept on the benches, which made getting a seat difficult. Ryan recalled how one guy was covered in newspapers and woke up cursing a man who accidentally sat down on him.

* * *

Ryan looked at his watch, and decided to make his way downstairs to the Bridgeport terminal on the New Haven line.

He reviewed his assignment objectives in Derby, and wished his Aunt Mary were still alive so he could visit her. She had red hair, a contagious laugh, and reminded Ryan of a younger Lucille Ball. She was his father's only sister and the only significant woman in his life during his youth.

Ryan slowly walked by the ticket information counter in the center of the terminal, and visualized where the bench seats used to be in 1967. It was here that Ryan had one of those impact experiences in his life.

* * *

Aunt Mary went to the ticket window with two of her friends, which left Ryan and the four girls behind with two of the mothers. The eldest girl, who was probably twelve, resembled Sally Fields from those old Gidget movies. She had a round face, dark hair, and a wide smile. Another was identical to Buffy on that TV show with the butler named Mr. French. She had blue eyes, yellow hair with curls, and a plaid dress. The third girl was another blonde who, a few years later tried out for, but lost the part of Jan on *The Brady Bunch*. She was pretty, but her lips drooped down, and this feature gave the perpetual impression that she was either sad or angry.

The fourth was the youngest; she had black hair, brown eyes, and was definitely spunky. She had purchased a Statue of Liberty souvenir at the gift shop in the park and had lugged it around all day long. The other girls had bought gifts too, but they gave them to their mothers to hold.

Anyhow, when Aunt Mary went to the ticket information window, one of the two mothers who were left guard over them, a heavy lady with a long red wool coat, decided to go off and buy a newspaper. This meant there was only one mother to watch over the five of them, and Ryan sized this mother up as shy and timid.

She was very frail looking, and exuded a peaceful disposition. Her hair was dark, she held her head straight with her shoulders back, and Ryan believed she was the mother of the little girl with the Statue of Liberty memento. She seemed especially close to Aunt Mary.

Well, for no apparent reason, the Jan Brady looking girl started to cry. During the day, each of the girls had cried about something: the cold, the walk, hunger, etc. Except the youngest. She never complained. It didn't make any difference to Ryan what their problems were, because he never conversed with them. To him, they were girls and lived in a different realm.

"I will never see them again, so why make friends? Besides, they are from Shelton and I'm from Derby."

* * *

Ryan smiled now at this logic, but as a young boy, these were good reasons.

Derby and Shelton were separated by the Housatonic River and connected by the Commodore Isaac Hull Bridge, within the region called the Lower Naugatuck Valley. Each city there was fiercely autonomous and tended to socialize along town borders, so Ryan's chance of even meeting one of these girls in the future was slim.

* * *

When the commotion started and the delicate lady tended to Jan Brady, Ryan decided to sneak off and find a toilet. He had needed to urinate ever since the walk from Rockefeller Center, and felt embarrassed to mention it to Aunt Mary in front of the girls. Ryan got off the bench, and walked in a direction he hoped would get him to a rest room.

He noticed that people looked at him as if they knew he was being disobedient and leaving without permission. They glared with disapproval. Two men, with beards and wearing long black coats shook their heads back and forth, but Ryan paid them no attention. He needed to relieve himself.

Besides, he was wearing PF Flyer sneakers, and the TV commercial proclaimed that they made you run faster. With this confidence, he pressed on and finally spotted a bathroom. Suddenly, a horde of people filed in and down the steps, bumped Ryan and turned him about until he was completely disoriented.

The four girls and the lady he had just been with, on the bench, were gone. They had disappeared. To Ryan it was as if God or the devil had taken them away. He was terrified.

All of a sudden, the grown-ups he walked past seemed different. Gone were the concerned men in the long black coats. Instead, one big fat lady laughed and pointed at him.

"Look. He's gonna cry." Ryan remembered her saying.

He didn't stop walking and prayed to God that he could find something that connected him with where he was supposed to be sitting. It was as if he had been transported out of Grand Central and to another train terminal in a far off place.

Sure enough, just like the big fat laughing lady said, Ryan began to cry. His face quivered, his arms shook, and the whole building seemed to spin in circles. Now his senses acquired supernatural ability. The roar of the trains, the station announcer, transistor radios, the tapping of feet, the snoring of people, and even the turning of newspapers were all heard like a crescendo to a symphony inside Ryan's young head.

* * *

Ryan got on board the train to Bridgeport and sat next to a window. He continued to think back to the time he got lost in Grand Central Station.

* * *

Miraculously, a man with a chalky complexion, wearing a white trench coat and a Fedora hat like his father's, approached him and spoke.

"Son, are you lost?"

Ryan felt relieved that some one was genuinely interested in his safety. He nodded yes to the man. The man reached out his hand to Ryan's, but before their fingers touched, a yell came out from in back.

"Mind your own business!"

It was Aunt Mary.

The man did not reply, but went over to a bench opening and sat. Aunt Mary grabbed Ryan by the arm and dragged him to where the girls were sitting.

* * *

As the train pulled away from Grand Central to Ryan's destination, a man, similar in appearance to the man he had met years earlier, sat down with a young girl in front by the exit door.

* * *

While Aunt Mary pulled him to the bench, Ryan looked back to see the guy in the white trench coat, but he was gone. Aunt Mary put him on the bench, and scolded Ryan for straying from the others. Abruptly, she sobbed, and tears smudged her mascara down her flushed cheeks. Ryan wanted to hug her, but was afraid the gesture was the wrong reaction for someone who caused the awkward incident.

The pretty and delicate lady came over and comforted her, while the girls looked at him. Ryan was amazed they did not stare at him with scorn, but instead with understanding. It didn't matter. From the fear of being lost, to the disappointment he caused Aunt Mary, Ryan again started to cry. His chest heaved and his breath shortened until the gyrations were too much for his ten-year-old bladder. It exploded. He peed all over himself and on the bench.

The Buffy girl, with the curly blonde hair, jumped off the bench to avoid getting wet, and leaped into the arms of her mother. At this, Aunt Mary cried even harder and came over and hugged him.

"I'm sorry. I'm sorry." Aunt Mary said.

It was evident right then that she understood why Ryan had left the bench, and she felt blame for the incident.

She took Ryan by the hand and led him into the women's room; then she waited outside the stall while he took off his underwear and pants. She washed off the pants with water from the sink, and handed them back under the gray painted stall for him to put back on. The underwear she washed and put into her red Naugahide pocketbook.

When Ryan came out, they hugged and walked hand in hand to the bench. The others were talking and paying no mind to him, but he still felt ashamed.

"Only little babies wet their pants. Everyone thinks I'm a little baby," he thought.

Ryan was humiliated. He sat on one end of the bench alone and stared straight ahead. He figured if he concentrated long enough, and made believe nothing bad had happened, and then everything would turn out all right. But it was all for naught. In his mind, he was the talk of the terminal. He was the little jerk. He was Pee Pee Boy.

* * *

Ryan smiled at what happened next, as the Metro North train rolled through Greenwich, Connecticut.

* * *

It wasn't long before the shortest, and the youngest of the four girls sat down next to him. Ryan could see her out of the corner of his eye, but he dared not turn her way.

She took his hand and held it in hers. Her hand was tiny, but somehow she was able to put her fingers through Ryan's and held tight. When it was time, they walked from that pee-drenched bench in Grand Central all the way to the train. They sat next to one another and stayed hand in hand. Ryan didn't look at her the whole ride home. When they had to switch trains in Bridgeport, she held his hand and led him to the platform and the connecting train. They didn't speak.

When the horn sounded, to warn passersby of their arrival in Derby, people started to gather their belongings. They never broke grip until the train came to a full stop, then she turned and gently kissed him on the right cheek.

Ryan watched as the little girl, with the black hair, took her bag with the Statue of Liberty souvenir, and walked off the train. She was probably six years old and he was ten.

* * *

Ryan looked forward to see the man with the young girl, but they were gone. Then, glancing out the window, he noticed a light flicker across the river on the approach to Derby, and what appeared to be a woman's figure waving. Soon it would be time to work; but for now, he had his thoughts and he remembered that little girl's kiss.

* * *

The kiss was genuine, and without the awkward tension of sexual expectations that come later in life. It was pure. And it was magical- like watching snow fall on a winter night.

For Ryan, it was the first time he had been kissed by a girl, and it couldn't have gotten any better than that one. It was special. The kiss was perfect.

Chapter 5

"Know how to hunt and you will be fed. Know how to sew and you will be clothed. Know how to fight and you will be protected. Know how to build and you will be housed. Know yourself and you will know the true nature of all things."
Translated from The Book of Lost Prophets*, Circa 200 B.C.*

As Sharma looked out the window from the room above her pub, The Brass Monkey, she was keenly aware of how wives must have felt years ago waiting for their husbands to return from sea. Were they lost? Did they find love in another woman's arms? Would they appear sailing up river to port with wide smiles and bulging cargo? Who's to know?

Sharma was now well versed in the history of Colonial Derby, and that the octagon shaped room on top of her establishment was called a "widow's walk," but she didn't need to be married to a sailor or a sea captain to understand its value.

For the last two years, her husband, Jack, had been distant. Although he was not lost at sea, Sharma worried she had lost him to another lover. Now, she feared they had lost each other, because she cared less and less about him.

The glass enclosed room, was large enough to fit one, maybe two-people, and Sharma determined that this was by design. There was a wooden cane backed chair facing south and a lantern that she guessed had not been used in one hundred years was fastened to a ceiling rafter.

Sharma was told it was lit at night so seafaring husbands could see their way home. She had put kerosene into it, but never bothered to test the lantern, so it stayed fastened to the top of the rafter. She could sense the spirits of women long ago, who entered this room to reflect and pray to God, and she wondered if all their prayers were answered.

Sharma sat down and looked out over the water. Then she took advantage of the solitude that the widow's walk offered. She thought about Jack and his gradual slide from her side. She thought about her parents, who were long since deceased, and she thought about herself.

* * *

Sharma loved sports growing up. This passion was a product of being the oldest of three girls born to a father who lived and died by his New York Rangers. Her father loved hockey so much that instead of coasters, hockey pucks were used at the kitchen table beneath drinks, and this much to the protests of Mrs. Gallo, who lived to arrange dinner like a Rabbi prepared for the Sabbath, everything was always meticulously placed. Mrs. Gallo always maintained that dinner was the one time that the family had a chance to bond, and her husband's antics took away from the hallowed ritual.

On Sunday, Mrs. Gallo would make linguine and clams from scratch, and then set the table with her china, only to have Ralph switch the coasters with the pucks. She had been given her coasters as a wedding gift from her aunt in Berletta, Italy. But now, round black rubber replaced them.

At first, it started as a joke, but then it became a tradition for him and Sharma. Mrs. Gallo was a defeated woman when it came to the New York Rangers and Ralph and Sharma's love of the team.

"At least I have two more daughters to dote on," she figured.

Mrs. Gallo understood that Sharma, being the firstborn girl and with no brothers, was her father's favorite. Sharma received the kind of attention usually reserved for a first-born boy.

From the time she was an infant, Sharma was on her father's lap watching the New York Rangers. Later, they would go skating, and she would pretend she was one of the players. When she was five years old, visitors would come and notice this beautiful girl walking around the house in a blue, white, and red Ranger jersey. She was always smiling and was never a problem, except when strangers asked the wrong questions.

"And who are you?" Ralph's friend from work had asked.

"I'm Walt Tkazcuk," Sharma would go into a hiss fit. "Who do you think I am?"

Walt Tkazcuk was one of her favorite players, and Sharma Gallo was at that tender age when a child's identity was not yet fully developed.

One time, Father Tiano visited when he had just arrived at Saint Joe's Parish in Saddle Brook, and he too made the grave mistake of asking Sharma her name.

"I'm Ted Irvine!" She screeched, and then proceeded to run and throw her body with reckless abandonment at Father, knocking him off balance and to the floor. Like Ted Irvine, Sharma spent a lot of time in the penalty box. She was constantly being sent to her room. After Father had left, it was Ralph's job to visit Sharma and scold her for her actions.

But all Ralph would say was, "Good hit."

Then he knelt and said prayers with her. He understood the passion inside of his girl.

When Sharma was six years old, Ralph took her into the city for her first live Ranger Game at the Garden. Years passed and she never missed a face off from then up to 1989. Weekend games she and her father drove in together, like old times, through the Lincoln Tunnel.

The Lincoln Tunnel signaled "show time" to Sharma. When they drove through the tunnel Sharma got a rush, because soon the skyline of Manhattan would be visible and the Garden was just a few blocks within view.

To add to her euphoria, leaded gas was still used and the noxious fumes trapped in the Lincoln gave her blonde head a buzz. She lived for hockey, and after years of attending Ranger games, Sharma became an integral part of the ambiance associated with playing at the Garden. Sharma was the "Angel" of Section 420 in the Blue area.

Now the Garden has section names like First Promenade, First Balcony and Second Balcony. Back then, the seats were painted like a rainbow, starting with red, then orange, yellow, green, and finishing with blue.

A blue seat was an inexpensive seat, and "the Blues" was a term associated with the beer drinking, profanity yelling fanatics, in the rafters. They were known for burning opposing players' shirts in effigy, and they were not to be mistaken for the stockbrokers in the red, or the yuppies in the orange, or the suburbanites who quietly sat in the yellow sections.

The cheap Blues seats numbered about 4,000. And each section had an "appointed" cheerleader who would lead their area in rendition after rendition of chants designed to insult the opposing players and referees, within binocular view below.

It was a blue-collar club that became quasi family to most of the regulars. Sharma was in charge of 420, but her nickname, Angel, had nothing to do with her good looks, and more to do with her demeanor; it was more in line with calling a great big guy Tiny or Pee Wee.

During week games, she would meet her father at the Blarney Stone, on West 32nd Street, for a few beers before walking over to Madison Square Garden. Some nights they met others from the 420 Section and socialized. Sharma "the Angel" knew practically all the names of the people in her section, about 400 in all, and their birth dates. For the older members of the Blues family, she held birthday parties at the Blarney Stone before games.

This particular night, October 1st, 1989, Sharma got out of work early from her secretary job at St. Thomas Press, which was located on the 16th Floor in the Flat Iron Building on Fifth Avenue. She hurried to the subway, took the green line up and then walked a few blocks to prepare for the quick celebration. She had streamers, balloons and Happy Birthday signs to display, because tonight "Tim the Tune Man" turned sixty.

The Tune Man was noted for a quick turn of phrase, and he created little ditties by taking a popular song and substituting words appropriate for the Ranger's game, like Weird Al Yankovic did making up satiric verses for the popular songs in his day. He became a virtuoso and was often asked for requests.

"Tune Man what do you have for McFerrin's, 'Don't Worry Be Happy?'" Someone asked.

He would make the appropriate adjustment to the lyrics, create a parody about that night's opponent, and then sing it.

Another fan would request, "How about Milli Vanilli's, 'Blame It On The Rain?'"

The Tune Man yelled back, "Ya mean, 'Blame it on the refs?'" Then he would sing a comical version, lambasting the referees using the rhythm of the Milli Vanilli song. And so it always went…

"How about Elvis's, 'That's Alright Mama?'"

"Tune, you know Sinatra's, 'My Way?'"

The Tune Man knew all the lyrics to the popular songs of the day, and the oldies too, and he gladly entertained his fans.

* * *

Sharma took a cigarette from her pocket and lit it. The sun was setting down river, and she looked at the reflection of the rays on the water. She exhaled some nicotine, and remembered the day when crazy Mrs. Adams visited the bar.

The old lady told Sharma a story about one particular week, and a night, she called the darkest in history, which changed the old lady's life forever. It was a story about lust and jealousy and greed and redemption, which she experienced as a young girl in Florida. The story culminated where she had to choose between riches or poverty. She chose poverty.

During that week, Mrs. Adams said, out of boredom, the forces of good and evil wager on certain lives and on the way they handle temptations. How these people responded, determined who won their soul.

"Derby is a safe haven from such forces, and that's why there still is such little crime here. No robberies. No rapes. No murders. No nothing. Derby can only be affected if a grave mistake was made to upset the balance. But the forces don't rush into town overnight. They prepare for their wager well in advance, so there will be signs."

When Mrs. Adams spoke, she suspiciously stared at people around her, like she had some kind of disorder, maybe a phobia, maybe schizophrenia.

"Besides, in the foothills, we have the book for protection. Those who have gone through this battle know that good and evil are brothers, sired by the same Father, but they won't fight in His presence, or in the presence of the book that He is writing, *The Book of Lost Prophets*."

Sharma nodded her head of thick blonde hair, took another cigarette from its pack and lit it. Mrs. Adams was long dead, but Sharma remembered the impact the old women's tales had that cold night.

"Remember, the same Force who created the man who would give you ten dollars tonight, created the man who will mug you and steal it from you tomorrow…" Mrs. Adams had said, then turned her head and yelled to a guy sitting alone by the window, as if he knew what she meant. "Right?"

She and Jack had just moved to Derby, and Sharma was mesmerized by Mrs. Adams storytelling. She was especially transfixed about the legend of that sacred book, passed on through the ages, which granted safekeeping from the force's games, to the town or host area where the book resided, and was read for all by a Nabi, or Prophet. As Mrs. Adams referred to them. They were the appointed "Keepers."

Sharma considered all that crazy Mrs. Adams said, and dismissed the stories as folklore or urban legends. But her point about one certain instance in life, which can affect your whole existence, was well taken, and Sharma thought back to the night of October 1, 1989.

* * *

At the time, the Rangers were in first place in the Patrick Division, so hockey was good. In fact, the Blues popularity was reaching celebrity status. George Plimpton, a regular at Ranger games, did a six page article on "My Blue Angel" that appeared in *Sports Illustrated*. It was a very favorable story and soon people were asking Sharma for autographs.

On this particular Friday night, at the Blarney Stone, about five people approached her for signatures on their copies of *Sports Illustrated,* which had just hit the stands out front. One of the fans was a giant of a man.

He stood about 6'7" tall, and Sharma found him very handsome. After she signed it, he sat at the bar and sent down a round of beers for everyone at Tune Man's party, which numbered twenty-five. Sharma nodded a thank you to him, and got on with the birthday celebration.

She proposed a toast, "Everyone, let's give thanks to the person responsible for us here today, Mr. Phil Esposito." There was a five second silence, and then a cheer for their General Manager and coach.

The Rangers were to play their hated foe, the Philadelphia Flyers, and Sharma's life would be changed forever. She knew that the new Ranger Management wanted a more wholesome image at the Garden, and this meant addressing the Blues.

Sharma gave up on buying shirts with her favorite players names screen printed on the back, and instead opted to have "Angel" embroidered across her Ranger's jersey. The player's jerseys were expensive, and her favorites kept getting traded, so Sharma figured she would save money by having her nickname instead. Besides, she had longer seniority with the team than any of the players and she planned on attending Ranger games for life, or so she thought.

The popularity of the Blues was on a track that was contrary with new management objectives, and Angel, by virtue of the Plimpton article, was its unofficial leader. So much so that VP Judson Perkins took her out for lunch in an effort to convince her that the new policy changes were in the best interest of everyone. It was a delicate matter as the Blues were the most loyal fans.

During the last twenty years, they had sold out the Blue Section for every single game. So, at the luncheon, Angel ferociously defended her Blues brethren. In her mind, there was nothing wrong with the way the Blues acted during games.

Management, she believed, acted like hypocrites, "On the one hand they loved our loyalty and money, but on the other they were ashamed of our conduct and appearance."

* * *

Sharma stood up from her chair when she heard the train coming into town. By now, it was pitch dark and the only light that shown was that of her cigarette.

* * *

Before the game against the Flyers, a message was heard by the public address announcer, which reverberated among the Blues like lightening striking a crowded swimming pool.

The proclamation was made that anyone caught standing in the aisles would be ejected from the game. The policy was really a ruse directed at the forty or so section leaders – like Sharma. Sure enough, when Sharma took to the aisle to lead her section in a robust cheer, two security men grabbed her.

Her 420 Blue Section family pounced on the security men, and a mini riot erupted. Police were called in, and the game was stopped. For half an hour, four fans held one security man by the ankles, over the railing, in negotiating a compromise on Angel's behalf. In the commotion, Ralph Gallo suffered a heart attack and died while pulling a policeman off of Sharma.

There was a time-honored tradition among the Blues that nothing of any type is thrown below. That night the tradition ended, and everything from beer cups, to popcorn, to cigars, was tossed below and onto the rink.

Sharma loved her father dearly, and one day, while boarding a train in Grand Central, she was inspired to immortalize the dark night her father died, after a friend pointed out to her two black tiles on the ceiling above the Northwest Passage area.

Way up on that gorgeous ceiling of hand painted constellations of the universe were two sooty tiles left untouched after the great renovation project. They were left there on purpose, as a reminder to everyone of what happens when things are neglected. Like a black spot on a lung x-ray, these tiles hung like an ominous relic of past neglect.

Sharma decided to get a tattoo on her left breast, with the date 10:1:89 inscribed. It was to commemorate the last game she and her father attended. And it was also a reminder of the corporate suits who harassed the Blues, and whom she deemed ultimately responsible for her father's death.

The tattoo was small; much like the ones depicted in movies that holocaust concentration camp victims have on their arms. And it was plain. There were no pictures or fancy colors, just that date in faded blue. It was personal. Close to her heart.

The time in the Blarney Stone before that fateful game, the large man who asked Sharma for her autograph was Jack Zawadski, the football player. He was in town with the Cardinals to play against the Giants, and he just happened to stop into the Blarney Stone for a sandwich before taking in the hockey game. Prior to walking in the pub, he bought a *Sports Illustrated* at the newsstand out front, and read the article "My Blue Angel" by George Plimpton.

When Sharma arrived, Jack had just listened to Mark Dillon, the brogue-speaking bar tender, brag about her. Jack was impressed and ventured up to get her autograph.

The next day Plimpton wrote another article about Sharma, and how Ralph had died at the game. The story about Ralph Gallo was headlines in three newspapers. Jack was at the game, but had no idea exactly who was involved in the melee up in the Blues, since he sat rink side. Jack read this article by Plimpton too, and he attended the services for Ralph on Monday night.

On Sunday afternoon, the Giants had destroyed the Cardinals 44-22. After a 13-year career, Jack was more or less a player coach, only he rarely played. After the following NFL season, Jack Zawadski retired.

* * *

The train turned the bend and headed to the station past the old "Narrows" shipbuilding cove, where Commodore Isaac Hull's homestead was once located. Sharma waited to see it. She glanced down and adjusted her bra, which hid her tattoo, then looked at the lantern. She reached up, pulled it down, and then lit it with her burning cigarette.

The lantern had not been lit in one hundred years, but now it was burning bright. Sharma had no idea why she lit it. Was it to signal her love for Jack? Was it a subliminal action, which meant something else?

“Did all those sailor’s wives, who waited for their husband’s love, stay faithful? Maybe they eventually used the lantern as a beacon for some new found lover, that the coast was clear to visit them? Who’s to know?”

Sharma doubted her love for Jack, as she waved to the six o’clock train, across the cove, when it passed by her home.

Chapter 6

"There is a traffic jam on the road to hell, so don't leave early." Translated from The Book of Lost Prophets, *Circa: 1957 A.D.*

The Derby train station was just as he remembered it, and not unlike many others he had seen throughout the nation. It was a one level brick structure with a ranch style roof, and a large red painted overhang. Ryan stood under it, and drank coffee he had purchased at the concession stand inside.

He collected his thoughts about his ex-wife Deidre, and decided he wanted a meaningful relationship. He would find a woman who needed him. Someone he could rescue from a bad situation and help turn her life around. Too often, in the last ten years, that was not the case.

He had always sought women for pleasure, now he wanted to find one to help. After all, he had the monetary means to do some good, so why not commit to a woman he could love, spoil and grow old with, and not just someone to use for sex.

Maybe it was the image of that little girl holding his hand years ago, or maybe it was a response to the pressure at work, but Ryan decided he would use today to start new. He would drink less, not seek purely sexual relationships, and try to focus more at his work.

The Brass Monkey was only a short two blocks away, so he resolved to visit Jack Zawadski, the ex-NFL player, and conduct business tonight. Ryan needed to purchase Jack's land for the trash plant to happen. So, he put his garment bag on top of his duffle and rolled the bags up the street. Putting pressure on his foot, Ryan discovered it was miraculously healed.

"An omen of good things to come," he believed.

After meeting with Zawadski at his bar, he planned to cab it to the Marriott in Shelton, and rest up for an early start the next morning. Ryan wanted to finish by the weekend and fly back to Cleveland for the Holidays to be with his friends.

When Ryan left Derby, the downtown was full of centuries old buildings; which, although old, were well kept. The streets were full of people visiting different stores and restaurants. Now, as he walked up Main Street, he couldn't help but notice the changes that had occurred.

Many of the older structures were still up, while half were torn down. As he turned onto Constitution Way, toward The Brass Monkey, he noticed a school of pigeons fly out from one building, all at once, as if they were being chased by vermin, probably rats.

Around 1972, a reporter had mentioned Derby while traveling through town on the way to a Jet-Giant preseason game. It was played at the Yale Bowl, in New Haven, seven miles northeast on Route 34.

"If you have never been in, through or around Derby, you are surely missing one of the great shattering architectural vistas of a lifetime," the reporter had written.

At the time, there was a big argument in town about redevelopment, and the article fueled the cause of people who wanted to tear down the old structures and construct new high-rise buildings. Even though the buildings were well kept: they were an eyesore to the more progressive people of that era.

That was the period of ranch style housing, butterfly roof construction, and strip malls. It was also the advent of Road Runner cartoons, Moon Landings, and *Playboy* magazines. Anything old represented stagnation.

The Valley loved football, and the dubious mention of Derby in the *New York Daily News* might not have been read at all, if it had not been in the sports pages. Ryan nodded his head, and thought about how 19th century period construction had come back in vogue. Regardless, Derby had changed from when he last visited. And the change wasn't for the better.

Ryan strolled the length of Constitution Way to The Brass Monkey. This was the property needed for the right of way, so garbage trucks could access O'Sullivan Island.

The inside of The Brass Monkey was brick; large exposed oak beams supported the ceiling. The bar itself was hand carved with gargoyle heads jutting out every four feet. The counter area was faced off with brass, a throw back to when the Valley was in its heyday as the "Brass Capitol" of the United States.

At the same time the Valley had this distinction, it was also known as the "Pin Capitol" of the world, and every August, during the "Old Ironsides" festivals, a boxing match between a hand picked brass worker, or brass monkey, and a pin worker, or pin head, highlighted the week long festival.

Five oversized ceiling fans were fastened straight down the middle, and helped circulate the cigarette smoke. The wall side of the bar, where they stored the drinks, came to a spiraled point, and was reminiscent of many gothic style churches constructed at the turn of the century. Also, there was, on top of the middle spiral, a brass monkey flexing its right bicep.

* * *

Three blocks away, Antonella DeLucia sat and thought about her dead brother Bobby. He had Cystic Fibrosis and had fought for every breath. Then, she thought of her mother, who toiled first in a mill and then in a rubber factory, only to die from cancer. She missed them, but was confident they were resting in the Forgiving One's arms.

Antonella also thought about the trash plant; she believed it was bad for people's health. She cherished every breath her brother and mother took, and believed the plant would cause cancer or respiratory problems for her neighbors.

But she was tired. Not from fighting the trash plant or from the hectic schedule the holidays brought. In the coming days she needed to make loaves of bread for friends, minister the Eucharist to the sick, make blankets to hand out to the poor, and attend meetings about the plant proposal. No, Antonella was tired of doing it alone.

Slight of build, she was an attractive single woman in her forties, but she had never met a man she truly loved. There were boyfriends a plenty, good and hardworking men, but no one who swept her off her feet.

She wondered if God wanted her to be alone. "Maybe my vocation is to be single? Maybe God wants me to be a spinster? Maybe I'll die one an old maid who finds comfort in the certainty of everyday habits? Who's to know?"

But if this was God's will, it certainly was not Antonella's. She was tired and she wanted someone to hold her when she felt scared. She was a woman and she wanted someone to dote on her every once in awhile, and make her feel more secure and appreciated. She was a strong woman, but she needed someone to stroke her hair, so she would have enough strength to face another day's battle.

Antonella looked out her window and stared at the moon. Off in the distance she heard the sound of the train whistle and thought about taking a trip into New York to visit Rockefeller Center and Macy's for the weekend, maybe even just a day. It was a twelve-dollar fare and she figured the trip could do her good. When she was younger, her mother took her there once a year. She loved it. It was big, exciting, and magical, everything the Valley was not.

"Who knows, maybe I'll meet a guy there." She imagined as she slipped off her pants and bra to put on her negligee.

After years of sacrificing her needs for her mother and brother, Antonella needed someone to care for her. She needed a man to hold her hand. Maybe someone who would run with her in an open field. She needed to be kissed, hugged, and caressed. She needed intimacy with a soul mate. She longed to feel a lover's heart beat against her breast, like their hearts beat as one.

She knelt to say her prayers, but tonight she said a prayer for herself. She was frightened. She sensed something strange was brewing within her. Something bad was birthing, and her thoughts were at war, so she petitioned God for strength.

Antonella asked Him to suppress her ego, for she knew that is where the source of evil loomed. She understood others were not as blessed as she, in suppressing their egos, so she needed to play her roll to the best for them. Every battle she won on a daily basis helped another who lost, she believed.

"All this has been revealed to me, so I am held more accountable," she mumbled as her head pressed against the soft pillow.

Her mother always instilled in her the adage, "To those that much is given, much is expected."

* * *

No music was playing when Ryan entered The Brass Monkey bar; so he walked to the jukebox, played a few renditions of Toby Keith songs, and sat on a stool.

The bartender was a short guy in his twenties, with stubby arms, and a large head, that was supported by no visible neck. He approached Ryan, and asked what he wanted to drink.

"A Diet Coke with lemon please." Ryan was determined not to consume alcohol.

The bartender looked bewildered when he served him, as if it was an odd request.

"Barkeep, do you expect Jack Zawadski to come in tonight?"

"Nope. Not tonight," the bartender answered turning away.

Realizing he had just wasted time walking to the bar because Zawadski wasn't there, Ryan looked at his watch. Then, looking around, he figured he'd buy the regulars a drink. Most of them were scruffy blue-collar guys, and they reminded him of his Uncle James, who was a machinist. His father was a blue-collar worker as well, but his appearance was different. He was always clean-shaven, and never wore his work clothes outside the factory.

After Ryan bought the bar a free round, each person waved thank you, then took turns approaching him and telling jokes.

"Hey, why did God give one more brain cell to a blonde than to a horse?" A big guy with a huge head, a white mustache, and protruding eyes asked.

"Hey, did you hear the one about?" A chubby man with a baldhead started…

No sooner did one person leave, did another greet Ryan, and engage him in a short conversation. There was the lanky guy who once worked in Clewiston, Florida, in the Eighties, crop dusting sugar came fields, when he was asked to crop dust for a company called WOD, over urban areas. He determined it was a top-secret chemical agent that strengthened our immune system, and linked the chemical to the increase in child ear infections.

After leaving the bar, the man returned, tapped Ryan on the back, and declared in a loud embarrassing tone, "We are in a biological revolution, Dude."

Another guy told Ryan how he was a back up drummer for the Average White Band and that they were planning a come back at Toad's Place in New Haven next year.

Another talked about a revolutionary basketball training device, called The Straight Shooter.

And yet another told how he worked at the Pentagon for five years, running the Luigi New York Italian pizza stand in the center of the courtyard.

"Yes, I was at the epicenter of it all," he smiled.

Ryan couldn't help but laugh. He had actually been there, and always thought that the stand was hilarious. At the Pentagon, behind five or so walls of fortified protection, was a New York Luigi Pizza stand. To Ryan, it was something he'd expect to see in a comedy scene from a Mel Brooks movie, or a piece lampooned in *Mad Magazine*.

"Never mind the oil, it's the pizza recipe we're fighting for right?" Ryan joked.

The man laughed too, and bought Ryan a Scotch on the rocks. Ryan had plenty of cash, and ordered another round when he noticed a man two stools away.

He was in his sixties and had a tattoo on his left arm that said USS something. He had a full head of white hair, a white beard, and wore blue Dickie jeans, along with an Ansonia High School football sweatshirt. He was talking to another man, of the same age, who resembled a caricature of a mobster. The man was short and dark.

The mobster looking guy had on black pants, black shoes, and a black turtle neck sweater. He was approximately 5'2" tall, wore a large gold chain, and combed his black dyed hair to the front of his protruding forehead.

Ryan sipped his Walker and zoned in on their conversation. The white haired man was telling his friend about transporting an out of commission destroyer from Florida to Derby to use as a museum. He raised money, but a decision was eminent between Derby and another location.

The Navy questioned the feasibility of the plan. They were concerned the river was not deep enough and therein lie the point of the conversation – Navy personnel were arriving next week to take water depth readings.

"Mr. Salvo, is there anything you can do?" The white bearded man asked.

The mobster looking man, Mr. Salvo, sat and just nodded his head. Then he got up, shook the other man's hand, and left the bar. The white haired man, with the tattoo, looked in the mirror and drank his beer.

Ryan understood the question was headed nowhere. He got involved with an asphalt plant in Detroit a few years ago and he knew the problem with the request.

Mr. Salvo most likely was in the asphalt and gravel business, and in order to be in that business, you needed to dredge riverbeds. In order to dredge, permits are required to work a certain area. The town gets involved, the state gets involved, and so do the EPA, inlands and wetlands commissions, etc. It is an extremely complicated process.

Ryan knew that in order for Mr. Salvo to dredge the river deep enough for a Navy Destroyer to come up the Housatonic, from Long Island Sound, he would have to move his equipment to the center of the river. Doing this could be a financial debacle to his company – if caught. A large fine could be levied and his permits would be pulled. Essentially, Mr. Salvo would be out of the asphalt business.

* * *

For fifteen minutes, Ryan checked out a woman sitting alone at a table drinking. He couldn't catch her name, but she was popular and even got behind the bar to pour herself a drink, when Sal, the bartender, went to the kitchen to check on an order of chicken wings.

She was a blonde, yet was very Italian looking: high cheekbones, full lips, angular nose and large brown eyes. Ryan put her age at thirty-five to forty, and she had a very athletic figure with large breasts, bulging out from a black top, which was not buttoned all the way up.

Ryan had another Walker, and then made eye contact with the woman. She slowly turned and walked in his direction. Ryan knew he was "the mystery man" at the bar, and that made him appealing. Men wanted to know where he came from and what he did for a living, and women were curious about the same things.

"Is Charlotte in the Carolinas or Florida?" One man asked.

"You work for General Motors?" Another inquired.

Ryan always felt bad not telling the truth, but he deemed it was important to always build a fake bio when on assignment.

Before the woman made it to Ryan, two things conspired against them talking. First, a guy from over by the pool table yelled to her. "Hey you want to shoot a game?"

She stopped, looked at Ryan, and then she turned to look at the man holding the pool stick. When she turned back a second time in Ryan's direction, a little man jumped onto the bar stool next to him.

Ryan smiled. He thought about what had just occurred in terms his father would use. A guardian angel intervened on his and the woman's behalf, so nothing sinful would evolve. That is how his father would describe the situation. But Ryan was not his father. All Ryan saw was a pesky man with a pool stick beating him to the mark with a good looking woman.

She turned and walked to the pool table.

Ryan bought another drink for himself, and one for the man who just sat next to him. His name was Nunzio; he was about 30 years old and had just come from a bachelor party. His friend, Gianni, had a sister who was getting married, and the stag was for her future husband.

Ryan was a little buzzed now, as he listened to Nunzio talk about the party for Gianni's not so future brother in law. Apparently Gianni hated the guy his sister, Ann Marie, was engaged to marry.

Nunzio didn't speak with an accent, but he had all the Italian expressions Ryan was familiar with growing up in an ethnically diverse area. As he spoke, he had his hands in the "praying position" on his chest. In rhythm, he would lift one hand up and then bring it down to touch the other in the praying position. Then he lifted the opposite hand up and subsequently brought that hand down to the same position as well. He repeated the process, again alternating each hand.

There was always a one second delay between each sentence for dramatic effect, and his descriptions were dispersed with racy slang like "chooch" for fool, or "pallinas" for testicles, or "cousin" for friend, or "kanoppers" for breasts, and "dong" for penis.

Nunzio said the groom to be was a big jock in high school and beat the crap out of Gianni every chance he got. He would play dirty tricks on Gianni, like slapping a "Homo" sign on his back, and sometimes he would push him into the girl's bathroom, and do other stupid things like that, which made school a living hell.

"A dog shits too much in the same place; he's bound to step in it, right?" Nunzio shared his words of wisdom with Ryan.

Nunzio said he and Gianni believed the guy was a big lady's man; Gianni knew in his heart the guy had not changed and would probably treat Ann Marie badly. So, Gianni decided to do what he could to break off the marriage and he offered to organize the bachelor party.

He was able to get 200 people to attend the Adriatic Marchigian, or AM, Club hall, and play poker, drink and eat, and, of course, view the customary stripper who was hired for the entertainment of the boyfriend. Nunzio named the guy "ass wipe."

As planned, Gianni coordinated it so that Ann Marie would come in right at the correct moment and see her fiancé being danced around by the stripper.

"Wa-wa," Ryan stuttered.

"What?" Nunzio interrupted.

"Easy for you to say. Yes. What if he didn't fall for the bait?" Ryan asked.

"That's the point. It was a test. If he fell into the temptation, no matter how well accepted, it would prove he had not changed. If he didn't fall for the set-up, then Gianni would know he was a changed man and good for his sister."

"But you are calling him ass wipe, so he must have failed," Ryan said.

"Cousin, let me finish the story."

Ryan listened as Nunzio told his tale. "Sure enough, a gorgeous stripper arrived and started to tease all the men. The stripper was dressed like a mummy, and was wrapped in white gauze like material from the neck down. The 'entertainer' then went over to the boyfriend, and kissed him on the lips."

"That wasn't his fault." Ryan blurted.

"Cousin, sure enough, but listen."

"The boyfriend, being a piece of shit," in Nunzio's words, "passionately kissed the entertainer. Then the stripper gave him a section of gauze to hold, and spun around until two giant breasts were exposed. Next, the stripper moved closer to him, and "ass wipe" started to suckle the giant kanoppers, as people applauded."

"You're right, he is a piece of shit." Ryan said.

"Sure he was cousin, but so was everyone there. We all would have done the same, but Gianni wouldn't want any of us to be Ann Marie's husband either. Gianni was like a father to Ann Marie, and he is very protective of her."

"Fair enough," Ryan said.

Nunzio explained that at the point where the boyfriend suckled the "kanoppers," is when Ann Marie walked into the hall, as planned. Nunzio said he noticed her, because he was tipped off, but no one else did. "Ann Marie was devastated because the boyfriend portrayed himself as beyond such childish behavior. Again, "Ass wipe" pulled the tape more, and the entertainer turned, exposing her naval. The boyfriend bent down and licked it. He was acting like a big pig. I didn't know Gianni had it in him." Nunzio laughed, almost falling off his bar stool.

"Had what?"

"Cousin, the stripper turned around and around and around, and exposed…" Nunzio pointed to his crotch.

"Lower extremities?" Ryan offered, trying to be polite.

"Cousin, this stripper had a 15 inch dong and pallinas the size of grapefruits! It was half guy and half broad!" He laughed. Nunzio said, "The whole place emptied out in minutes. Men were running out of the hall knocking each other down to get out first. One guy jumped out the window, because the doorway was jammed with people. Another man was trampled, and crawled to the exit on his belly. A guy named Tony charged the stripper, only to be punched in his face by the shemale. It was total bedlam. Gianni set him up big time. Gianni had the last laugh!"

Ryan laughed and patted Nunzio on the back. "So, I guess he flunked the test?"

"Cousin, there is no way that ass wipe will be forgiven. There will be no wedding this Saturday at Saint Mary's."

Nunzio left shortly after telling his story and Ryan picked up the newspaper.

He found it interesting that the old battleship, the USS *Constitution*, was docked at Captain's Cove Marina in Bridgeport. Apparently, the ship was making stops along the east coast as a living monument for citizens to visit and tour.

The story mentioned that it was supposed to have docked at the Merchant Marine Academy in New York, but Senators Lieberman and Dodd somehow persuaded the Navy to let her dock in Bridgeport for a week.

Ryan had seen it in Charlestown, Massachusetts years ago, but thought it might be nice to visit it again if time allowed. His late uncle, Louis Beach, who was his Aunt Mary's husband, was somehow a distant relative of Isaac Hull, who was the ship's Commodore, and Ryan's father took great pride telling him about the family connection.

His father even won a grade school contest naming an old movie house after Commodore Hull. But then again, everything in the Valley was named after him: festivals, road races, streets, schools, theaters, and bridges were just some of the constant reminders of the Valley's favorite son, Hull.

After Ryan read the article, he turned to his right and the woman he had made eye contact with earlier, was sitting there.

She flicked her hair, took his hand, and asked if he wanted to dance with her.

Ryan determined she was some wife going through a mid life crisis or a divorce, and decided he didn't want to know her. Listening to Nunzio's story, he thought back to the temptations he and Deidre experienced, and determined again he would try to do better in that regard.

"No, thank you. I am a terrible dancer," he said.

She looked embarrassed, took a sip of her drink, then touched his thigh, "I really don't want to dance."

Ryan was attracted to her, but wanted no part of knowing the woman. He thought about Deidre, and the young man who had shot himself and the guilt he felt for that domino affect of marital bliss weighed heavily on his mind.

"Listen, I have to get to the Marriott," he said.

"I'll drive you," she offered.

"That's okay, a cab will be fine."

She laughed, and then looked into his eyes. "This is the Valley, Sweetie, the one cab company closed at ten."

Ryan was cornered, and accepted a ride from her to the hotel.

She stayed with him through the night, but left before five in the morning.

Chapter 7

"Hatred manifests itself in our very appearance. Bro show me a man full of hate and I'll see one ugly dude." Translated from The Book of Lost Prophets*, Circa 1667 & 1996 A.D.*

Ryan woke up Thursday morning at the hotel, ate breakfast, and asked for a lift to the nearby rental car location in downtown Shelton. Nina, the girl at the front desk, called an older gentleman who drove him there. After that, he wanted to go back to his hotel room to study his notes before heading to the Derby City Hall for his visit with the Mayor, Keith McHugh. The appointment was for 10:00 a.m., and Ryan wanted to be prepared. McHugh was the main reason Tony Scarpa gave Ryan this assignment.

He grew up with McHugh in the sixties and early seventies on a street referred to as Irish Main; Ryan anticipated this meeting with some anguish. He wanted the encounter to go smoothly, so he tried to bury any animosity he felt, from the past, toward McHugh. But it was difficult.

It was important to Ryan that he acted in a professional manner, so he ordered a pot of black coffee from room service, turned on his computer, and reviewed all of his notes regarding the trash plant, especially the section on Keith McHugh.

* * *

In the 60's of Derby, Connecticut, if you were Irish, like Ryan, you grew up on Olivia Street. The street went for three long blocks and on both sides it was a venerable Who's Who of Irish families.

In all, there were approximately fifty structures on each side of Olivia, mostly two and three family clapboard units, with several six family brick tenements, and three or four one family colonials. Every last person in the area, almost nine hundred total, was Irish.

Housing laws of forty years ago were non-existent so collusion or "steering" was commonplace. Congress enacted the Fair Housing Act in 1968, but the law was not vigorously enforced. So, Olivia Street neighbors made secret phone calls when a house was for sale, or a rent was available – to conspire so that another Irish family replaced the departing Irish family. For the most part, if your name was not of Irish decent, you were not living on Olivia Street.

The Irish, after decades of being in the majority, were on a decline to the Italians and Polish, and Olivia Street was their last stand. Once in a while, a family that did not have lineage from the Emerald Isle would slip through, but usually this happened because that family was thought to be Irish.

For Instance, one time Mr. Keefe told everyone he sold his home to the Moran family; but in reality, the family was named Muraze and it was from Poland. By doing this, a plausible cover name was established and the whole neighborhood referred to them as the Moran's. It made no difference they spoke with Polish accents.

* * *

Ryan saw the note that said McHugh was to receive twenty thousand dollars for his roll in the trash plant.

* * *

On Olivia Street, you had two types of leaders, the "muscle" leader and the "spiritual" leader. The muscle leader was Shamus McHugh, and he was the grandfather of Keith McHugh. If you were having a problem with the law or needed your son placed on the city payroll, or if you needed someone to be threatened with physical harm, old man McHugh was the person to whom you gave homage. The McHughs were the self-appointed chieftains of Olivia Street.

In all, there were ten McHugh families on the street, and the younger members patrolled it like storm troopers, especially where the Italian kids, who had just arrived and couldn't speak English, were concerned. They were called Genardos by the McHughs. Ryan believed this slur had been derived from the first Italian family who immigrated to the Valley in the 1800's, and the name became part of the local diction. Territory fights often occurred between the Genardos and the McHughs.

Genardos were allowed to walk across Olivia Street, at the different street intersections, but walking the length was regarded as a sign of defiance. Usually, before they could go from one block to the next, a posse of Irish boys would be there to instigate a fight. A McHugh always anchored that gang.

None of the McHughs were big, but they were tough, and each reminded Ryan of a penguin, by the way they waddled and always seemed to be chirping about something.

"Hey Genardo, speaka English?" Tim McHugh would say.

"Hey Genardo, I'm gonna screw your sister." Quinn McHugh would add.

"Hey Genardo, got any olive oil?" Another would yell.

And so it went…

Trash talk like that was always being recited by a McHugh and it was always to trigger a fight.

* * *

Ryan thought about Old Man McHugh and how, when he died, the Mayor and the Bishop both spoke at his funeral and both preached about how good and honest a person he was. Ryan got up, opened his steel brief case, and found the money envelope with Keith McHugh's name on it.

* * *

Olivia Street had a spiritual leader too, and that person was Ryan's father Bill Walsh. He was the person you sought guidance from when it came to religious matters that you didn't feel comfortable revealing to a parish priest, or the issue was so spiritually debilitating, that you sought uplifting wisdom to get you through the difficulty.

Ryan knew the story of his father's youth. When Bill was in his teens, he worked at a grocery store for a Jewish family named Pransky, and they treated him like family. In particular, Mr. Saul Pransky was very close to Bill. He encouraged him to read the Kabbalah and the Talmud, and Bill read them just as much as he read the New Testament in the Bible. Bill reflected on the link between the Hebrew prophets in the Old Testament, he called Nabi, and his devotion to the Catholic faith, or so he tried to explain to Ryan.

"The Jewish, Christian and Moslem faiths are all intertwined." Bill would yell out to Ryan. Ryan was the only person around, and confiding in his son was Bill's only outlet to share a new found "truth."

"Ryan, let me read to you from Nabi Amos and tell me what you think? Ryan, have I ever told you about Nabi Ezekiel? Ryan, Nabi Isaiah says this…" and so it went.

He was always finding something new about God and the Nabi he was studying. Later, he read parts of the Al-Qur'an and mentioned to Ryan about God's revelations to Nabi Muhammad.

"All three faiths preach peace and love to one God! There are many rooms in God's mansion Ryan, why quibble over which floor? I'd be happy in a broom closet."

Ryan always paid attention to his dad and he enjoyed the expression of wonderment on his face when he poured through his books. Besides, Ryan needed to listen to him, because Bill was always listening to someone else.

Often Ryan would come through the front door and find a man or woman in the kitchen, confiding in his father. Sensing they wanted privacy, by their low tones and body mannerisms, Ryan would go straight to his room. Bill never mentioned to Ryan about his conversations, and Ryan never asked.

* * *

One time Ryan came home to find their insurance man crying on Bill's shoulder, and Ryan couldn't resist sneaking around through his bedroom, into the living room, and listening.

Mr. Steinberg's son was close to death from cancer, and Mr. Steinberg was near suicidal.

"I can't live if Jeffrey dies. Help me," he cried.

Ryan watched as Bill recited a psalm to Mr. Steinberg, and told him not to lose faith. He reassured Mr. Steinberg that there was a heaven, and that one day he would be united with his son Jeffrey.

"How do you know Mr. Walsh? How do you know?"

Ryan saw his father look at the man, the way he often looked at him, and say, "I just know. All I can tell you is I just know."

The confidence and sincerity Bill Walsh exuded startled Ryan. To him it was as if God were speaking through his father. "In a way, my dad is a Nabi too," Ryan mumbled.

The Steinberg's were Jewish, and one month later Ryan and Bill attended their home for Shiva. Jeff had passed. Ryan was ten and he had never been to Shiva, but he had been to two wakes. Sitting low on the parlor couch and eating pastries, he looked around and noticed all the mirrors were covered.

To a young Catholic boy, the customary avoidance of one's reflection to forsake vanity was never practiced, so the white sheets that surrounded him, on the mirrors, on the picture frames, and on the china closet, made him tremble.

He looked for his father, but he was nowhere to be found. What made him more fearful was the sight of Mr. Steinberg and the other men. They were unshaven, and each wore torn white shirts as if they had been in fistfights. To add to Ryan's discomfort, he was sitting in a room with all women. And all the men were in the next room reciting prayers in a foreign tongue, he had never heard.

* * *

As he turned onto Howe Avenue in Shelton, Ryan knew now Mr. Steinberg and the other men's appearance was traditional for Shiva, and that the prayer was the Kaddish and it was said in Hebrew or Yiddish. But back then, the prayer seemed to have the speech patterns of some satanic chant, or some ghoulish movie sound track from Creature Features he watched on Saturday nights, and the tones scared him.

* * *

When it was time to leave the Shiva, Mr. Steinberg hugged Bill, and gave him a gift.

"My grandfather wanted you to have this, but I disobeyed his wishes. Now I know why it belongs to you." Mr. Steinberg presented Bill with a book. "Shalom."

"This means so much to me. I loved your grandfather. He was a father to me. Shalom," Bill said.

Ryan remembered the book was written in long hand, and was bound by leather reinforced with cardboard, that was laced with raw hide strings, much like the ones used on Indian Moccasins. The parchment cover was tanned yellow, with the title, *The Book of Lost Prophets*, on the front in red.

* * *

Ryan turned onto the Isaac Hull Bridge toward Derby, and remembered it was at Jeff Steinberg's Shiva when he learned that Mr. Steinberg's grandfather was Mr. Pransky.

Mr. Pransky, who was his father's mentor at the grocery store, instilled in his father a passion for spiritual enlightenment through parables and expressions, which were always passed on to Ryan.

As he looked to his right at the river and noticed dredging equipment set up only twenty feet from the Shelton side, Ryan recalled one Jewish expression, which his father taught him that he felt especially applicable to his meeting with McHugh.

"Ryan, if you have the least doubt about someone, hold him in esteem, as you would a Rabbi, but watch him as you would a thief," he would say.

Bill Walsh would never speak badly of anyone, but Ryan could tell his father didn't like the McHughs.

* * *

Keith McHugh was two years older than Ryan, and became the President of his senior class. By that time, his nickname was "Thief McHugh."

Whether it was organizing a bus trip to an amusement park for the neighborhood kids, helping out with the summer church festival, or selling "salutes" for the fourth of July celebration, McHugh always handled the money and many believed he pocketed more than his fair share. It didn't surprise Ryan that he was involved with his clients; it did surprise him that McHugh was the Mayor of the city.

Ryan parked in front of the Derby City Hall, which doubled as the Veterans Memorial Community Gymnasium. The ground level was a community pool with a workout area and the second floor had a basketball court, which Ryan frequented every Friday after school to shoot hoops.

Adjacent to the gym were the city offices: treasurer, tax collector, town assessor, city clerk, and the mayor's office.

Ryan approached the office and noticed a lady with her back turned filing charts into a cabinet, so he knocked on the open door. She turned with an annoyed expression on her face.

"Yes." she said.

"I would like to see Keith McHugh."

The lady put the files down. "No one sees the Mayor without an appointment."

The manner she said it reminded Ryan of the overly protective sentry who guarded the Wizard of Oz at the entrance to Emerald City. She was quick tongued and she seemed mad. He imagined her next utterance to be, "No one sees the great McHugh, no way, no how," and then slam the door in his face.

Ryan paused slightly, "I… do have an appointment." By slowing his reply, Ryan made certain he didn't stutter.

"And you are?"

"Tell him Ryan Walsh is here."

The lady picked up the phone, in the tiny office, and announced his arrival. Before she hung up, the door flew open and there stood McHugh.

Keith "The Thief" McHugh was in his fifties now, and Ryan tried not to laugh. McHugh was decked out in a black suit, and had an unlit panatela in his mouth. Coupled with his short height and inherited waddle, McHugh looked like a penguin now more than ever. And an ugly penguin at that. McHugh had a large mole on his left cheek, which Ryan remembered from childhood, but now it had two whiskers growing out from it.

"Ryy-ann." He bellowed, and then moved forward to embrace. "How long has it been? What, seven or ten years?"

It was nine years ago when Ryan had tried to avoid him at a Michael Jordan's restaurant in Chicago. Ryan said nothing, then patted McHugh on his shoulder and proceeded into his office. McHugh slammed the door and then pointed with his cigar hand in the door's direction.

"That bitch break your balls, Ry? She's my girlfriend's older sister. She needs to get laid!" He yelled at the closed door.

Ryan saw that there was a mirror on back of the door and was happy his hair was in place and that he had not cut himself shaving. Then he looked over the room and noticed there were pictures of McHugh's children on the walls; framed in black were two boys, who looked like McHugh, and a girl who had blonde hair and pretty light blue eyes.

McHugh sat behind his desk and a picture of President Kennedy hung on the wall behind him. Ryan sat in one of the two red leather chairs and looked at him. He could detect smugness in McHugh as he folded his hands and sat back in his leather chair.

He knew Ryan from childhood, and to McHugh, Ryan was the son of an eccentric man, who amounted to nothing. He had no idea what Ryan had accomplished in the past thirty years. The fact that he graduated from Dartmouth, or that Ryan had traveled the world on several occasions was never a consideration to him.

Ryan decided not to engage McHugh in conversation. He remembered an adage his father told him. "You don't throw your pearls before swine."

To Ryan, Thief McHugh was a swine. He reached into his blazer, pulled out an envelope, and handed it toward him.

"Slow down partner," McHugh said pulling back in his chair.

Ryan pulled back with the envelope, took out the money, counted twenty thousand dollars, and placed it on his desk. Keith started to talk, but Ryan waved him off by putting both palms in front of him.

Ryan Walsh knew that Keith never respected him growing up. They both just happened to be from the same Irish neighborhood. Walsh understood fully that if he had been from another ethnic group, Keith probably would have beaten him in his youth.

Abruptly, Keith ran to the door and locked it. His face went limp as Walsh put the money back into the envelope, and placed it in his stubby hands.

"Why be so bold?" the Mayor asked.

"What is there to be fearful of Mayor?"

"What we are doing is illegal."

"Is it? In that case Mayor, maybe we shouldn't do this."

"You know what I mean. We can't let anyone know." Keith tried to reason with him. "Why are you testing me?"

"If it's a test Keith, you already flunked. Just take it."

Keith had a smirk as Walsh spoke. He counted the money with his hands beneath the office desk.

To Walsh, the Mayor seemed nervous and gave off the traits of a quivering schoolgirl about to make it for the first time. He had Keith in his pocket now, but he didn't really need him. All that he required was a simple majority vote from the Board of Aldermen, and the rights to The Brass Monkey.

Walsh considered Keith "The little Mayor of Munchkin Land." He had no legislative voting rights, and gained power only through influence. He was needed should there be a tie vote, in case the one swing vote decided to abstain, then he had the power to break the tie and that was all.

Walsh spent the next fifteen minutes asking Keith a few questions, and learned there was an aldermen meeting that night. The TR Trash Plant was not on the agenda, but it would probably be discussed in the public portion by a grassroots group called P.R.I.D.E., which opposed it.

"If anyone asks McHugh, I am just an old neighborhood guy passing through. No one is to know why I am here." Walsh said this standing over Keith for dramatic effect.

"Okay Ryan, okay, whatever you say."

Walsh purposely said nothing, then turned to leave, saw his reflection in the mirror on the door, and noticed a large red pimple had formed on his chin, probably from the stress of the last few days. He hid it from view, with his left hand, as he walked past McHugh's secretary.

Chapter 8

"Before the battle, the brother forces meet and embrace." As Translated from The Book of Lost Prophets, *Circa, 700 A.D.*

Thursday, Sharma woke up with the realization that a decision to change her life had been made. She had been angry about the trash plant, and frustrated about her husband's love, which seemed lost, but she had kept herself busy by staying active volunteering in the community.

For awhile, helping to coach in youth sports, and the countless hours she spent fundraising for different causes, diverted her discontent, but now this seemed to fade, and Sharma wanted more in life.

She believed she had more to give. Financially, she and Jack were well off, but that satisfaction meant little. Lately, she found herself drinking more, and was irritable when dealing with her regular customers.

She found herself asking, "Is this it? Is this all I have to look forward to day in and day out?"

So, she decided not to wait any longer for Jack's love. "It is what it is," she concluded. Nor would she fall victim to the townspeople regarding her property. She was determined to strike out and take what was hers in life. Yes, she would stay married to Jack, but that didn't mean her emotional well being had to depend on his love.

Last night she crossed that divide. She met a man and slept with him. The guilt, which chained her, and prevented her from committing this act a year earlier, suddenly seemed to loosen and fall off. She saw the world differently now.

She seemed invigorated, like she was driving to a Ranger's game, with her father, through the Lincoln Tunnel to watch them play the Flyers. She didn't know what lie ahead for her, and she didn't care. Sharma was excited. The rush she felt made her feel strong and confident enough to tackle any problem that confronted her.

She showered, dressed in jeans, combed her hair, put on her makeup, and decided to phone Nell to see if she wanted to visit

New York for the day. She knew Antonella had the next two weeks off, from her nursing job at Griffin Hospital, and she thought it might be fun to bring her to New York and show her the city.

Maybe they would walk Chinatown and purchase "knock off" pocket books on Canal Street, or take in a play, or eat at Sardi's Steak House, or just visit a bar like the Blarney Stone and have a few drinks. Whatever they decided to do would be fine. Sharma was full of energy and needed to vent.

* * *

At 6:00 a.m., Antonella woke up tired. She was haunted when she slept by a strange man, but it was unclear what the vision meant. Her mother always told her that the future sometimes appeared to people during sleep.

"Antonella, the Almighty often speaks to us in dreams," she would say.

"Sure enough, didn't God warn Joseph in a dream to flee to Egypt?" Antonella reminded herself.

But what did this dream mean? Was it truly a premonition or just a dream brought about by anxiety and the need to rest? Then again, didn't Kings of old have dream interpreters in their court? Antonella could not decide. Who was this mysterious man? Was he the father, she never knew? Was he someone she would meet soon? Was this man good, or was he evil?

All these questions rambled through her head. She was tired and had a lot on her mind, so she put her concerns in the hands of the One.

Antonella showered, dressed in jeans, a white wool sweater, combed her wavy black hair, put on her lipstick, and had a sudden urge to call Sharma.

When she went to bed last night, she thought it might be good to take the train to New York for the day. Maybe she needed to get away, and see a change of scenery. She walked out of her bedroom, and into the kitchen toward the wall mounted telephone, but before she got to it, the phone rang. It was Sharma, and she wanted to meet.

They agreed to take the train to Grand Central in Manhattan, so Antonella walked down to The Brass Monkey to meet Sharma. She still felt strange and light headed. She wondered if she was getting sick, or maybe going through menopause. Antonella knew she was not the correct age for such a change, but the thought actually comforted her.

“At least that would be an explanation for my restlessness,” she mumbled. Antonella could deal with that easier than she could with the conflict in her heart.

As she approached The Brass Monkey parking lot, she noticed Mayor McHugh getting into his car. It was too late for breakfast, so she wondered if the Mayor was there to talk to

Sharma about the trash plant, and the businessman who was coming to town from Cleveland. "It's really none of my business. He has a right to talk to Sharma, and Sharma has the right to listen." Antonella accepted this fact as she opened the door to the pub, and greeted Sharma who was leaning against the bar.

They hugged each other, and kissed opposite cheeks.

"Are you ready?" Sharma asked, tying her blonde hair back in a tight ponytail.

"Yes, I'm ready. A little tired, but I'll be fine." Antonella sighed, putting her hand over her mouth.

"Nell, I'm glad you wore sneakers. You'll need them to keep up with me."

"I might be small Sharma, but I have a lot of heart. I'll keep up with you."

"We'll see," Sharma's brown eyes stared into Antonella's.

Antonella glanced down.

Chapter 9

"Fear of the unknown, makes man a coward, fearlessly attacking the unknown makes man a fool, embracing the unknown with the known makes man wise." Translated from The Book of Lost Prophets, *Circa, 37 A.D.*

Ryan remembered reading an article in the *Connecticut Post* last night that the USS *Constitution* was docked in Bridgeport at Captain's Cove Marina. It had nothing to do with the trash plant, but Ryan was always amazed that when he took pleasure trips, he often bumped into people who could be of service to him down the road. So, he decided to drive the short distance and visit the USS *Constitution*, always with a trained eye to meet someone he could use.

Ryan left McHugh's office knowing he had everything under control, so he drove south down Route 8 and phoned Tony back in Cleveland to give him an update, but all he got was voice mail.

He left a message, turned on the radio and listened to "Sweet Home Alabama" on FM 108. It was an "Oldies" station and Ryan instantly recalled the first time he heard the song: he was driving on this very road to Bridgeport.

That time, Ryan was in high school, and had to drop off a part for work at a machine shop. He did a favor for his boss, and drove his old Dodge Dart there for the first time. Although Bridgeport was only seven miles away, and the largest city in Connecticut, Ryan had never been there before and he got lost. What made the trip memorable was that it rained in torrents, and the car stalled out after the distributor cap got wet going through a deep puddle.

The section Ryan was stranded in was a "colored" area, and the only black people Ryan had ever seen were depicted as criminals on television, so he was nervous. He got out of the car and walked across the street toward a bar to seek help, when he noticed there were ten African American teenagers on the corner looking at him.

Instantly, they reminded Ryan of the McHughs on Olivia Street in Derby, and Ryan saw himself as an unsuspecting "Genardo" off the boat from Italy.

His heart beat rapidly as he anticipated being jumped, but he opened the door to the bar unharmed and relieved he had made it that far without being harassed. Looking inside, he froze in his steps. Every person in the bar, The Magician Club, was black and they stopped talking and stared at him. The place was instantly silent. Ryan stood in the doorway and decided what to do next. If he walked out, he would offend the people at the bar and be at the mercy of the gang at the corner. If he went inside, maybe he would never walk out.

* * *

Ryan drove slower down Route 8 toward Captain's Cove.

* * *

He remembered a cliché his father sometimes used, "There is no such thing as an atheist in a fox hole."

So, he prayed to Jesus, to Mary, and to the mother he never knew. He prayed for protection from these "colored" people he didn't even know. Ryan was in that proverbial foxhole his father had mentioned.

He took a deep breath, walked in the bar, and the steel door closed behind him. He was eighteen, which was the legal drinking age, so he sat on a stool and asked for a beer.

Everyone turned his way as the bartender, who looked like the deposed Ugandan dictator Idi Amin, with a round black face and bulging wild eyes, served him.

* * *

Ryan saw the sign for the Route 25 connector, now named the Colonel Mucci Highway, which led to Interstate 95, and Captain's Cove. He was five minutes away.

* * *

One minute into the Magician Club and Ryan's worst fears were realized. A man approached him and asked for five dollars. Ryan had no choice, but to acknowledge the man straight on.

"Sir, my car is broken down outside, and I work part time in a rubber factory. I need money much more than you," Ryan paused, "I was hoping you could give me five dollars."

With that, the bar erupted in laughter. One man yelled to the guy soliciting the money and told him to leave Ryan alone.

"He might be dangerous. He might be some crazy vigilante like that Charles Bronson actor from that '*Death Wish'* movie ."

Everyone laughed again. They knew Ryan was no vigilante.

* * *

Ryan turned onto Interstate 95, and stayed in the right hand lane so that he could take the Fairfield Avenue exit to Captain's Cove. He fondly remembered that day he got stranded.

* * *

He spent two hours at the Magician Club bar not paying for a single drink. One of the men told him to wait until it stopped raining and he would get the car running, and he did.

* * *

When a commercial came on the radio, Ryan remembered the man worked for FM 108 in advertising. He was a former University of Connecticut basketball player, and gave Ryan his business card. Ryan exited the highway and turned left onto Fairfield Avenue, when he recalled the best part of that day.

* * *

He sat at the bar, being the only white person with about thirty black people, when the door flew open. At the threshold were two white men, in their late twenties, deciding whether to enter or not. They were caught in the same dilemma Ryan had been in earlier. And again, the bar was silent. They turned and left. They were too afraid to come inside.

At that the whole place erupted with choruses of "Boo! Boo!" Ryan found himself joining in too and yelling, "Boo!" As if that were not enough, he waved his hands in a "get lost" gesture.

"We don't want your kind here!" he said.

* * *

Ryan followed the signs to the marina and remembered a saying his father often recited. “When all else fails, pray for enlightenment.” Ryan could not get his father’s teachings and sayings out of his head.

Aside from actually seeing him, it was as if he were still alive, actively trying to communicate with him. Ryan held back tears. There was so much he wanted to tell him; but didn’t, and he wished there was some way he could. But he knew there wasn’t. His father was dead.

* * *

Ryan was very familiar with Captain’s Cove. Although it was in Bridgeport, it was also in Fairfield County. In all, Deirdre and Ryan lived about fifteen years in Fairfield County, and they found comfort in the fact that their neighbors were just like themselves. They were upwardly mobile, educated, and wealthy. Living there gave them a feeling that they had “arrived.” In Connecticut, Fairfield County was the posh place to live.

Phil Donahue and Marlo Thomas, Paul Newman and Joanne Woodward, Rodney Dangerfield, Don Imus, Jack Welsh, Donald Trump, Dustin Hoffman, Arthur Miller, Henry Kissinger and Martha Stewart, were just some of the celebrities you stood a good chance bumping into if you lived in Fairfield

County Connecticut, and Ryan and Deidre took pride in this fact. They lived among the rich, the famous, and the influential.

Two friends they socialized with were Ursula and Jonathon Tinker. They were just a few years older than Ursula and Jonathon, so they did everything together on the weekends. Jonathon was a lawyer like Deidre, and Ursula was the offspring of doctors. She was afforded all the opportunities in schooling and social mobility, which Deidre, Jonathon and Ryan were not. She attended the Gunnery Preparatory School and later Yale University, where she studied drama and was roommates with Jodie Foster.

When Deidre and Ryan knew them, Ursula still dabbled in acting, but her desire for success on stage, was just not up to the challenge. She would partake in local theatre and from time to time do poetry readings at the Historical Society, but most of her energy was funneled into causes.

Save Long Island Sound, A Woman's Right to Choose, Habitat for Humanity, and Save the Rain Forest, were some of the organizations she helped out in.

When Jerry Brown ran in the Democratic Presidential Primary, Ursula was already one of his campaign organizers in Connecticut two years before the election. And guess what? Ryan nodded his head. Brown won Connecticut, beating a candidate by the name of Bill Clinton.

Ursula kept Deirdre, Jonathon and Ryan very busy. And she was the type of person who would not take "no" for an answer. Even if someone did say no, the word wouldn't compute in her busy brain.

That's how Ryan volunteered at Captain's Cove Marina, to help reconstruct a replica of an old British Frigate, christened the HMS *Rose*.

* * *

Ryan turned into the marina parking lot and remembered the weekends spent here nailing planks, sanding boards, and applying protective coatings to guard the ship against the harsh salt water elements.

* * *

In the beginning, Ursula, Jonathon, Deirdre and Ryan worked just about every other weekend. Then Ursula went on to another project, next Deidre stopped coming, and finally Jonathon hung up the hammer. Ryan was the only one who kept working.

Ryan knew it was not by coincidence that Jonathon quit a week after Deirdre, but he didn't care. Working with his hands, that year was one of the happiest times in his life. He felt fulfilled seeing something being created out of nothing.

When the ship was completed and launched into Long Island Sound, Ryan felt like a proud father watching his baby take her first steps. To this day, Ryan has a picture of the *Rose* hanging over his office desk back in Ohio.

A few years after the *Rose* "cause," Jonathon and Ursula divorced, and Ryan never saw them again. He did see the *Rose* though. One time in Savannah, Georgia, while enjoying a beer at a River Street tavern, Ryan noticed the *Rose* docked out front. Like meeting a long lost loved one, Ryan ran to her.

As it turned out, she was sailing up and down the East Coast, embarked with a replication of the Magna Carta. College Students attending Sacred Heart and Fairfield Universities in Connecticut were on board. They paid for a three-month summer voyage and were receiving college credit for the experience. Ryan half expected to see Ursula Tinker on the *Rose* that day, but she wasn't, and Ryan remembered feeling relieved.

When he parked and walked to the pier to see her, Ryan found it interesting that the USS *Constitution* set about the same voyage as the *Rose*, but she wasn't there either.

* * *

Then it dawned on him that the cove would be too narrow to dock the USS *Constitution*. It was approximately 200 feet long and housed 500 Navy men in her day, whereas the *Rose* was a much smaller class frigate. She was used for transportation trips to shore and for scouting.

Ryan noticed people standing in line and looked out to sea to spot the USS *Constitution* anchored probably a quarter mile out. The people were waiting to board a tugboat, which transported them to the ship. Ryan decided to order a clam roll and beer, and he sat indoors, where it was warmer, and looked out over the cove and marina.

Captain's Cove Marina was located close to a low-income housing project and across from a capped landfill. Trees and bushes were planted on the landfill, and you could hardly tell it was seething with methane gasses and carcinogens – all leaching into Long Island Sound. Ryan knew that it had once been a dump, so the illusion that it was a small hill was lost on him. It was a landscaped landfill to Ryan.

That aside, he was impressed to see that the marina was thriving with little shops made to resemble an old colonial village, and they sold tourist items like pocketbooks, flags, clocks, candy, and books.

He was sitting there about fifteen minutes when the guy who operated the tugboat sat down across from him. He was about sixty and had a white beard, reminiscent of pictures he had seen of the writer Ernest Hemingway.

He was a little overweight, and his pants and sneakers were old and torn. He ate a hotdog and Ryan noticed his hands shake as he put the dog up to his mouth. His eyes were bloodshot and his nose was a road map of blood vessels.

A minute went by when Ryan decided to speak. "You're keeping pretty busy out there."

The man looked up and nodded his head. Ryan glanced down and noticed a tattoo on his forearm that said, USS something. Ryan couldn't make it out, but he remembered having seen it before, when he realized this was the same man that had been at The Brass Monkey just last night. This was the white haired guy who had talked to the mobster looking guy about dredging, and bringing a naval ship to dock at O'Sullivan Island in Derby.

"Sir, I noticed your tattoo. What does it say?" Ryan asked. But when he pronounced tattoo Ryan stuttered, and the word came out, "ta-ta-too."

The man looked up, "The USS *Hull*."

"Wow, what are the chances you should be working aboard the USS *Constitution*? I mean Isaac Hull being its Commodore and all?"

At this, the man opened up to Ryan, and they had a nice conversation. His name was Dan Izzo and he served during the Vietnam War aboard the USS *Hull*.

It was a Forrest Sherman-class Destroyer, and Dan's tenure was from 1967 to 1969. The ship was deployed to perform shore bombardment missions along the south coast, and in the Demilitarized Zone during 1968.

Ryan told Dan that he was from North Carolina, but originally from Derby, and just passing through. Dan mentioned to Ryan he too was raised in the Valley. He graduated from Ansonia High School, and then enlisted in the Navy. Upon completion of his service, he owned an auto body shop for several years, but sold it.

"I had a friend who worked for the Bridgeport Harbor Authority, so here I'll guide the *Crack of Dawn* until I die," Dan paused, "that's the name of my tugboat."

"My name is Ryan."

"My friends call me Tugboat Dan."

They shook hands as the Metro North train rumbled south toward Manhattan on the tracks in back of them, just past the parking lot.

* * *

Not much later, Ryan departed to the Valley along a secondary road called Route 110. It was commonly referred to as the River Road, because it meandered along the gorgeous Housatonic River. As he turned a bend, Ryan noticed a "Tag Sale" sign in front of an old colonial styled home, and recalled how he had entrusted all of his possessions with an estate liquidator when he left Derby.

He wondered if any of those possessions had made their way to the tag sale circuit, in particular, he thought about the book that Mr. Steinberg had given his father. His father had always kept that gift in the center of his bookshelf. It was not a book that was ever left on the kitchen table.

"Maybe *The Book of Lost Prophets* is being sold there? Maybe, it is being passed from one flea market and tag sale like so many old relics? Maybe I'll travel down some road in Nevada or Tennessee, and find that book some day?" Ryan entertained these thoughts, but knew he would never try to find the book.

He drove past Sikorsky Aircraft, where the Black Hawk helicopter is manufactured, and saw O'Sullivan Island in Derby approaching. He thought about Tugboat Dan and his plan to have a Naval Destroyer moored there, and he felt bad that Dan's idea would be crushed. Ryan liked Dan, but his goal and Ryan's mission where at opposite ends. "Anyhow, a guy like that is waiting to have his dream snuffed out, right?" Ryan thought.

Ryan turned left toward the hotel. It was then that he noticed the dredging equipment, he had seen earlier, had been moved out to the center of the river.

Chapter 10

"The scorpion's bite isn't always deadly, but it is always toxic." As translated from The Book of Lost Prophets, *Circa: Unknown.*

Antonella sensed a change in Sharma's demeanor as they rode the train through Bridgeport, past Captain's Cove Marina toward Fairfield, and south to Manhattan and Grand Central Station. Her eyes seemed distant, trance like, and her smile forced. Antonella said a prayer for Sharma, hoping that whatever was bothering her would be lifted. She often prayed for others, it was a habit instilled by her mother.

"Antonella, when you see someone poor or suffering, say a prayer something good will come their way," her mother Josephine would say.

Lately, she questioned the worth of prayers, and her intentions. Was it sincerely for the other person, or was it a habit employed for her own peace of mind? If the prayers were for her own peace, then wasn't she selfishly praying for herself? Wasn't that wrong? And how about her prayer's value? Did they ever work? She didn't see any miraculous transformations in her life, certainly not where her brother or mother were concerned.

"Maybe I'm a fool? Doesn't God love us no matter what? If so, why be worried about doing the right thing all the time? After all, is He perfect? Look at the war in Iraq. Look at 911. Didn't He have a hand in that by not intervening? Didn't He commit a sin of omission?"

Antonella was tired. But she held onto the "truths" that had been revealed to her in the past, as if they were refreshing raindrops. She couldn't even remember the last time a "truth" had been revealed to her, but she drew on the faint memory that one did years ago.

"What's the alternative? Everyone knows evil works overtime to confuse souls. So, until I am shown otherwise, I may as well hold onto the ways I have been living."

She felt excited again about her trip to New York. "Who knows, maybe I'll meet a guy there. Maybe my dream will be revealed. Maybe I'll have a name and a face to go along with the outline." She thought.

She sat and glanced out the train's window. Suddenly, she saw Sharma's face reflecting off the glass, and it startled her. The image was distorted, and had no eyes. Antonella turned and smiled at her, and Sharma's brown eyes looked back.

* * *

Sharma was restless. She looked at Nell, and, for the first time, was disgusted in her. No longer did she see a pretty and wholesome good person, whose company she enjoyed, but a weak and superstitious woman, who let her opinions about right and wrong handcuff progress. Mayor McHugh had told her that a nice offer would be made to her husband, and Sharma was determined they'd accept.

If the money was good enough, she could buy a beautiful home in the suburbs and live without having to greet small-minded neighbors every day. She wouldn't have to listen to drunks say they loved her each night, or the latest rumors about lottery winners. Nor would she be subjected to crazy tales, like the one about the forces of good and evil, and the power of some mysterious holy book, hidden in the foothills, from an old eccentric like Mrs. Adams.

To Sharma, the Valley was on a downslide. She observed what was happening. Homeless shelters were being shut down everywhere except in the Valley. This meant drug addicts and sex offenders were finding their way to Derby, because Derbyites were the only people stupid enough to still have a homeless shelter.

These homeless people were not even Valley residents, but the shelter was a so-called non-profit and accepted state and federal money, so it had to accept anyone. Once at the shelter, they were legal Derby residents and put into the Title 19 system. To Sharma, these people were deadbeats.

Sharma witnessed these scams before in Jersey, and knew the Valley was being turned into a dumping ground, full of losers. Now, as she glanced at Antonella, Sharma wished she hadn't asked her to go to New York.

"What happens if I meet a guy there? I couldn't do anything with her by my side. It's like having my mother with me."

* * *

They arrived at Grand Central and walked to Times Square, then ate lunch at Bubba Gump's, before walking toward 45th Street. There they noticed the Naked Cowboy, in the middle traffic island, playing his guitar in white jockey shorts. Like schoolgirls, they giggled while having their picture taken with him as a souvenir.

After that, they walked up 7th Avenue past Rockefeller Center, stopping in boutiques along the way, and toward Central Park. Sharma was cold and complained about the walk, so they ducked inside a bar to have a beer and rest.

* * *

"Antonella, when was the last time you were with a man?"

Antonella was thrown back by the question, and her face blushed. "What?" Her reply was more scorn than a question.

"No, seriously. When was the last time you were with a man, Nell?"

"Really, Sharma, are you serious?" Antonella said, her eyes now looking down.

Sharma knew Antonella was not comfortable talking about such matters, but she didn't care. She wanted to bridge a conversation so she could tell Antonella about her affair last night. She knew Antonella would never divulge her secret to anyone, because gossiping would be considered a sin to Antonella' heart.

Sharma wanted her to know. She was curious to see how Antonella would react to her tale of lust. Would she like it? Would she change the subject? To Sharma, Antonella was the perfect person to tell, because it would go no further. And in a strange way, although it was she who had intercourse with another man, by telling Antonella, it was like she was in bed with the stranger, too.

Antonella tried to concentrate on other things, while Sharma told her the particulars in explicit detail: her salad, the waiter, the waitress, the Mickey Mantle clock, the weather, the sweater she bought in a boutique on the walk, but it was to no avail. She had to listen to Sharma.

"When I say he was big, I'm talking thick, too. Can you picture that Nell?"

Antonella could indeed imagine what she meant, what woman couldn't? But, she felt uncomfortable and after fifteen minutes was determined she had heard enough.

"Enough Sharma! You are getting me all…."

"Hot?" Sharma smiled.

"Flustered. C'mon let's go."

Sharma was happy she had told Antonella about the affair, but she could sense her confession did not have the affect she wanted. It was only 3:00 p.m., so Sharma suggested that they take a taxi across town to see her uncle Jasper, who tended bar at a restaurant called IL Vaga Bondo.

"Okay Sharma, but don't forget we have to catch the six o'clock to get back for the aldermen's meeting."

Sharma nodded her head, but she knew she was not going to any more meetings about the trash plant. "Of course," she said.

* * *

IL Vaga Bondo is on East 62nd between 1st and 2nd Avenues, and it looks like a residence to the average visitor. Formerly a brick row house, the restaurant has black shutters on the windows, and a short front courtyard enclosed by a black wrought iron fence. Only after walking down a few granite steps, did Antonella notice an aluminum stamped plaque identifying it as, IL Vaga Bondo, to the right side of the wood door entrance.

The front section is a bar, and the dining is to the rear. In the summer, the outside bocce courts are busy with older Italian guys in fedoras and young businessmen on break. Sharma's uncle Leo Vagnini-Jasper is the bartender there most weeknights. Except tonight. Tonight Jasper was a patron.

Sharma spotted Jasper and went over and hugged him. She introduced Antonella, and the three grabbed a table in the bar section and ordered drinks. Antonella noticed Sharma was back to her old self, and seemed to be at ease listening to her uncle with the white hair and handsome features.

Antonella was also enjoying the visit and was entertained as Jasper went from one story to the next. First, he told a funny story about Sharma's mother and himself living in Italy, and then he told another about his older brother, Vincenzo. He was a horse trainer at Saratoga in upstate New York, and before that, at Thistledown in Cleveland, and Hialeah in Florida. Next, he told another tale, which Antonella and Sharma listened to intently.

When Jasper was a newlywed, he had his own paint contracting business. He did this for four years before deciding to call it quits. Apparently, he had quoted on a big job worth 20K, being a sub contractor painting several city owned office and school buildings.

"Back then, that was a great sum of money, and, if everything went as planned, I would have enough to invest in better equipment, a new truck, and a down payment on a two family in Flushing, Queens."

The problem was that every time Jasper went to get paid by Mr. Miko, the General Contractor who hired him, the man had an excuse not to fork over the money. "I just deposited it today, come back tomorrow. Did I say come here today? I meant next Monday, because the bank messed up and put it into the wrong checking account."

On some occasions, the man would stoop so low as to fake the death of a family member. "Jasper," he would whine, "my aunt died and I can't discuss business today, you understand." Other times it was the standard: "I just mailed your check yesterday."

Jasper told Sharma and Antonella that he began having trouble paying his help and borrowed money just to keep his business solvent. After a few weeks, he began to get stomach sickness and developed gastritis. The pain was so bad he walked hunched over everywhere he went. To church, to the bar, dancing with his wife, you name it, and Jasper bent over trying to relieve the pain that afflicted his intestine. Next, Jasper figured he would get an ulcer.

Finally, he could no longer bear the torture being cheated caused him, and he said "enough." He threatened the man with legal action, and since the work was bonded, this meant Jasper could pull the bond, and Mr. Miko took this seriously.

"All of a sudden Miko had a conversion of conscious, and cut me a check for the balance owed, which amounted to $15,568.00." Jasper lifted his hands in mock imitation of a traveling faith healer.

Jasper walked to the Bowery Bank, where both he and Mr. Miko had their accounts, and asked the teller if there were sufficient funds to cover the check. The teller, who was Jasper's cousin, Linda, looked the account up and discovered Miko, was $100 short. This meant the check would bounce.

"He's at it again, I figured. He thinks I'm a fool."

Trembling from frustration, Jasper dropped the pen that was in his hand on the bank's marble floor. Then, when he bent down to retrieve it, an inexplicable idea came into his skull.

"The revelation was so powerful that, when I stood upright, the pain in my stomach disappeared."

Sharma and Antonella laughed as Jasper reenacted the whole scene in animated detail.

"Here's what I did. I had $100 in my pocket and deposited it into Miko's account. Then I asked Linda to cash the check he gave me. I lost $100, but got $15,568.00 in return. In short, I cut my losses, and then I decided to get out of the business."

"Uncle Leo, what made you ask how much was in his account?" Sharma said.

"Sweetheart, in the back of my mind I had a feeling he would try to trick me again. Then, I remembered an Old Italian expression my father, your grandfather-told me. It goes like this, *il lupo perde il pelo ma non il vizio*." Jasper slowly pronounced the phrase in Italian.

Sharma put both her hands up, "What?"

Then Antonella chimed in, "It means the wolf will shed its hair, but never its habits."

"Hey, close enough. We have a real *pisano* here, huh?" Jasper laughed, and patted Antonella on the shoulder.

Sharma and Antonella laughed as the waitress came with another round of drinks.

At that point, Sharma asked Jasper how her cousin Lisa, Jasper's daughter, was doing. His shoulders went down, his eyes moistened, and his chin stiffened.

"Not well," he paused long enough to control his emotions, "Lisa's husband is a compulsive gambler and he owes a large sum of money to the local loan shark," Jasper sighed, "I've tried everything, from giving them money, to getting him counseling, but nothing I've done has worked."

"Uncle Leo, maybe you can ask one of your friends to talk to the loan shark?" When she asked this, Sharma had the enthusiasm of a naïve young girl. And Antonella was reminded of the purity still in Sharma's heart.

"It's too late kid. I knew it was too late last week when I visited their screen-printing business for ten minutes. When I came back out to my car, all the windows on both their vehicles were smashed. My car was left untouched. This meant the Mob was casing Lisa and John and sending them a final message."

Jasper looked down. "Last night they signed ownership of the business over to the shark and promised to work it free for six months. My daughter is basically a slave." Tears ran down his tanned face.

"All because of an asshole like John," Sharma nodded.

"He's not a bad man Sharma," Jasper spoke with a tone of resignation, "he has a bad problem."

"Still, Uncle Leo, I can't believe he couldn't change if he really wanted to change."

Jasper wiped his eyes, then sat up in his chair, and pointed his right index finger at her, "Honey, remember what I told you earlier?"

Sharma did not know the answer to his question, and stared with her mouth half open.

"*Il lupo perde il pelo ma non il vizio*. The wolf, will shed, its hair, but never, its habits." He spoke the English translation in two word blocks.

Shortly after this, they parted ways with Jasper, and hailed a taxi to Grand Central.

Antonella did not speak a word when Jasper told the story about his daughter, but concentrated on Sharma and Uncle Jasper's opinions.

To Antonella, Sharma seemed to suggest that the son-in-law could overcome his problem, if he chooses to, but he didn't. Jasper seemed to profess once you have an addiction, you can never overcome it. Antonella believed anyone could overcome a problem, but that they sometimes needed help.

They arrived at the station, and caught the six o'clock back to Derby. Once on the train, Sharma turned her back, and didn't talk to Antonella. Antonella again said a prayer.

Chapter 11

"The questions of the eternal are vast and complicated. The answers must be whispered into man's skull. Be careful, the force of good, and his brother, the force of evil, each have tongues." Translated from, The Book of Lost Prophets, *Circa: 215 A.D. & 1942 A.D.*

Ryan woke from an afternoon nap, and went to the lounge to get a sandwich and a beer. He was focused on his mission to solidify the trash plant deal, so he put a call into McHugh on his cell phone. He needed to see one of the aldermen who would be a swing vote for the proposal, Joe Romanzo. Joe was a high school classmate. Keith answered the phone and told Ryan it was all set for them to meet at 3:30, on O'Sullivan Island.

Ryan drank his Heineken, and checked the inside of his blazer to make sure he had the money envelope to pay off Joe. From the time Ryan knew Joe, he had always been an honest person. Ryan was curious to find out why he had become corrupt. What pushed him over the edge?

* * *

In high school his nickname was "Joe Nosepickum," at first, and then it was just "Pickum." Kids can be cruel and Joe was the example of such cruelty. Apparently, he acquired the name in the 8th grade at Lincoln School, where he was frequently spotted picking his nose in class, and the alias took.

Ryan never saw Joe picking his nose, but he did see him blowing it. No matter where he was, Joe would sneeze his brains out, and that's why he always had a handkerchief in his left hand. In the classroom, in the gym, in the lunchroom, name the place, and Joe Pickum was forever blowing his nose.

Joe stood about 5' tall and had very short arms and lazy eyes. He would speak to you, but never look in your direction, and this gave the impression that someone was sneaking up on you when you spoke to Joe. Half the kids called him Pickum, and the other half called him "Roman Eyes," for the obvious reason, his eyes always roamed. And it was a play on his last name.

Most students in high school have nicknames, and, if you are lucky, they are good ones. The Nud, Sully, Beegs, Iz, Condor,

P-Row, Kodiak, Raven, Greek, Balls, Boomer and Kal are all prime examples. If you are not so fortunate, you get hit with a bad one, but that's where it ended.

Well, Joe won the lottery of nicknames and they were all bad. To complicate matters, Joe also had a gigantic nose. So some kids, who didn't know Joe at first, got it all mixed up and called him "Roman Nose," because they figured his nose roamed all over his face too.

* * *

Ryan ordered another beer. He thought it was sad that Joe had to be paid off, but he didn't think it was odd that Joe was an alderman; Ryan knew Joe before he became corrupt.

* * *

To the outsider it would seem unlikely that someone with three negative nicknames like, Nose Pickum, Roman Eyes, and Roman Nose, would ever have the self-confidence to run for political office. Most people would figure by looking at him, that Joe was the type of person who was teased so much his ego was stomped out of existence, but not Ryan. To Ryan, Joe had the type of good traits you wished to see in all people.

Ryan recalled how one day a group of numbskulls tore the blouse of a freshman girl in the hallway by accident. They were horse playing and the wire spirally thing, that holds the paper together in binders, got caught on one girls shirt. She was a pretty Polish girl named Wanda something. Then, as the boy ran to get away from the others, his spiral binder in hand, the blouse came with him.

There stood this shocked young girl with her bra exposed for all to see. It was the first time Ryan had seen a bra "live" so his memory was vivid on this episode. He stared at her the whole time. Joe was there too, but he took his tee shirt off in seconds flat and gave it to her to wear. Ryan didn't think of doing that; he was too busy gawking at the girl.

Joe was one year younger than Ryan, but they hung around on and off in high school. Ryan wouldn't describe them as best friends, but they were chummy.

One day Ryan had Joe over to his house to watch the Ken Norton and Muhammad Ali bout on TV. Ryan's father was home and watched it with them, as they ate pizza, drank cola, and listened to Howard Cosell call the fight.

Ryan's father really liked Joe, and remarked to him when he left, "Ryan, that Joseph is a wonderful young man. He's the type of person who would give you the shirt off his back."

Ryan was somewhat embarrassed. His dad was not in the hallway when that young girl's blouse got torn off, so he had no way of knowing what had occurred. Ryan certainly didn't tell him, because he was ashamed of his own behavior. But Bill

Walsh was a good judge of character, and Joe Pickum would give you the shirt off his back. In fact, when tested, he did.

* * *

Ryan left the hotel after finishing his beer and drove to meet Joe. He turned onto Elizabeth Street, and then Minerva, but he felt troubled about their meeting. Ryan was used to appeasing slime balls, the types who justified payoffs and free trips to Aruba as a cost of doing business, but he never figured Joe would be one of them.

He turned right onto the Caroline Street extension, went through the old wooden train overpass, past The Brass Monkey, then underneath the Commodore Hull Bridge, and waited for Joe on the island.

O'Sullivan Island is not exactly an Island; it is a peninsula. It's where the Housatonic and Naugatuck Rivers join and then flow to Long Island Sound.

This section was considered the head of the tidewaters. The DEP called the area an Estuary, where salt-water fish like blues, flounder, and striped bass, intermingled with fresh water fish like carp and pickerel. And because the tides affected the area, the island was often submerged during the rain season.

For years, the island was the site for the Cotter Firemen's Training Facility. Two three story concrete buildings were lit on fire and then extinguished. This was to simulate a fire response, and to prepare the volunteer firemen on procedures and safety precautions. However, with the new environmental laws, this method became outlawed, and the training facility was overgrown with brush and trees.

It reminded Ryan of one of those *Indiana Jones* movies, where the actor, Harrison Ford, happens upon a lost ancient pyramid or village right under everyone's nose. The firemen's training school was not discernable. This land was forgotten and abandoned, and this made it an ideal location for the TR Energy Plant.

* * *

At 3:45, a large white van approached and parked next to Ryan. On the side window was a handicap sticker, and Ryan figured that if that was Joe, he had a job in the school system transporting children. A man got out of the van and stood by the driver's side door. The man was completely bald. It was Joe.

He was short and stout with large black eye glasses. He wore a denim shirt, with corduroy pants, and work boots. Ryan got out of his car to greet him and expected his demeanor to have changed, but it hadn't.

"Ryan, it's great seeing you. You look great. How are you?"

Ryan noticed he had his signature handkerchief in his left hand when they extended greetings.

"I'm doing fine Joe. How are you?"

Joe's roaming eyes were the same as he had remembered, and meeting him alone under the circumstances of an illegal payoff, reminded Ryan of some espionage novel, where the police, or an assassin, waited close by to pounce on them.

They stood between the two vehicles where no one could view them and talked for twenty minutes. Ryan told Joe a little about himself and Joe told Ryan about his life.

Joe worked at Sikorsky Aircraft nights and during the day at the Home Depot. He married Wanda, the pretty Polish girl he gave his shirt to in high school, and they had a daughter, Maria. She was thirteen years old and in the 7th grade.

Ryan inquired about the van Joe was driving, thinking he had yet another part time job. He speculated that Joe was in debt with charge cards, or else purchased a home that he struggled to afford. To Ryan this explained Joe's need to be paid off for his alderman's vote.

"The van is for Maria, Ryan."

"I don't understand Joe. Why do you need the van for your daughter?" Ryan asked, and then realized his question was self explanatory, and he felt embarrassed.

Joe went on to tell him that Maria was injured when she was seven years old and confined to a wheel chair. Worse is, Joe explained, he caused the accident when he played football with her in the backyard. Joe played on his knees, while Maria played standing up.

At one point she ran with the ball, and he gently pushed her, but she stumbled and slipped off an embankment, fell five feet, and landed on her neck-breaking it. Joe said Maria needed another operation to help with her breathing passage and the insurance company would not pay for the procedure.

"Joe, under the circumstances I would do the same thing as you." Ryan stammered on the word circumstances, in his zeal to comfort Joe for his actions.

Joe turned his head down slightly and looked at Ryan. This was the only maneuver Joe could employ to stop his eyes from moving, and he did this whenever he wanted to make a firm point to anyone.

"I hope you would do the same. I would die for my child."

After that, he took the envelope from Ryan, said goodbye, and left the island.

* * *

Ryan was left to ponder what had just occurred. Mostly, he tried to reconcile Joe's predicament in his head.

"Was Joe right or wrong taking money for his daughter? And what kind of God would put someone in that position? Joe had to choose between being a thief, or his daughter's life. Who could pass such a test?"

Ryan looked at the area he was purchasing and justified, in his mind, that without his arrival to solidify the TR Energy Plant, perhaps Joe wouldn't be in a situation to get money for his daughter's operation.

"Maybe, I was sent here for the reason of saving that girls life?" Ryan considered.

But as soon as he thought this, Ryan realized it was a delusion. There was no guarantee Maria's life would be saved. Even if she lived, what kind of life is it being in a wheelchair?

Ryan drove down the dirt road, which led out of the island, to the paved road where The Brass Monkey was located, and decided to have a drink and see if Jack Zawadski was there. He wasn't, so he drove back to the hotel.

His mind was still on Joe Romanzo, when he remembered a parable his father told him in grade school. It was about four friends who brought a paraplegic on a mat to see Jesus. When they got there, the building where Jesus preached was so packed with followers that they couldn't gain entry.

"The four friends had such faith Ryan, that they cut a hole in the roof and lowered their paraplegic friend down before Him. Jesus told the paraplegic to rise up, take his mat, and leave. His sins were forgiven and he was healed."

Ryan thought about the parable. "Weren't they breaking the law? Wouldn't cutting a hole in the roof of a building to get Jesus' attention be wrong?"

Ryan parked his car.

"Maybe, what's not told is that their paraplegic friend was healed, but the four friends all went to jail. Wasn't Joe doing the same thing? Wasn't he breaking man's law, so his daughter could live? Wasn't he saying enough of your rules to the world? Who's to know? Who's to judge?"

Chapter 12

"Like exploding aerosol cans, the end of days comes with entropic energy. It appears the universe has slipped into chaos, but I assure you man, it has not. Suddenly, dude, you turn and notice the ACME moving van about to mow you over, like a dumb coyote in the desert." Translated from, The Book of Lost Prophets, *Circa 1973 A.D.*

Sharma stepped off the train without saying a word to Antonella and walked home to The Brass Monkey. She grabbed a bottle of wine, went to the widow's walk, and sat. It was eight o'clock and usually dark, but today it was bright. It seemed daylight savings time came early.

It was so clear, she could see the smoke stacks, from the Keyspan Power Plant in Port Jefferson, New York, about fifteen miles across Long Island Sound.

She always despised seeing them. To Sharma, the two stacks were filthy and menacing, situated so close to the water where the ferry from Bridgeport ported in the little harbor town. But now they appeared friendly.

The more Sharma thought about Antonella and her neighbors in Derby, the greater her determination was to see identical stacks from the trash to energy plant on O'Sullivan Island. She wanted the best possible offer for her property and she was determined to do anything to get it.

Although it was nearly Christmas, the weather was unusually spring like and had not yet dipped below 50 degrees. Derby was at the center of a fault line for New England weather to the north, and mid-Atlantic weather to the south. Often, during snowstorms, one side of Main Street would get snow, while the other side received rain. During the April shower season, the south end would be sunny, while the north end poured rain in torrents.

That's why Sharma wasn't surprised when she noticed a cloud moving up the Housatonic River from Long Island Sound, toward the town.

Many people from outside the region, remarked how unpredictable the weather conditions were in New England, and she knew the Lower Naugatuck Valley region had the most erratic changes of all.

Sharma watched as seagulls, which often flew up river to scavenge for food, headed further north toward Ansonia and Seymour. Looking across the cove, she noticed the Conlon's bulldog, Chunk, run for cover under their side porch as the dark cloud settled. Soon Sharma expected to hear the roar of thunder, but there was nothing, just a dark cloud.

Yet, as she turned toward the parking lot, she noticed a guy covering his head with what appeared to be a notebook, as if against rain, but she saw no precipitation. Sharma opened a window to investigate by putting her hand out; and, sure enough, it was raining. She could feel cold pinches, like hundreds of needles, against her flesh. Oddly, when she brought her hand back inside, it was dry.

"Only in the Valley, can it rain dry," she thought.

"Sharma are you up there?" A man's voice called.

It was Todd, who usually tended bar during the day for her.

"Yes, Todd, I'm here."

"There is a guy asking for Jack, but I told him you were here. Do you want to speak with him?"

"I'll be right there," Sharma said.

She had an idea who it was, because the guy was a stranger to Todd. It probably was the man from Cleveland, and he was here to make an offer. Sharma looked down river at the smokestacks on the Long Island side of the Sound, one last time, before night came, and they disappeared from view.

"Maybe my ship has come in?" She smiled.

* * *

Back at the Marriott, Ryan went to the lounge to have a drink, and then called Tony back in Cleveland. He let Tony know about his meeting with McHugh, as well as his attempt to see Jack Zawadski, and the successful meeting with Joe Romanzo.

Tony told Ryan that TR Industries was prepared to go as high as two million for The Brass Monkey property, but that an incentive was in place. Besides their standard seven per cent cut, they got the difference below one million. Tony wanted Ryan to offer $500,000, and said that he would receive a twenty percent commission, as a bonus, from $500,000 to one million. The property was assessed at $250,000.

After talking with Tony, Ryan thought about the incentive. He wasn't concerned about the money pay out, but he wanted to secure the deal as close to Tony's goal as possible, out of principle. This way, he would show that he produced. By offering and securing the least amount, he could prove to himself, and to Tony, that he still belonged in the agency.

He walked to the parking lot, and got into his car. Backing out, he noticed storm clouds coming in from the southeast, and figured it would rain soon. He didn't have an umbrella and intended to stop and buy one, but drove past the first store he saw. In ten minutes, he was crossing the Hull Bridge and noticed the dredging equipment hard at work in the center of the river. For some bizarre reason, it was still light enough to work.

He turned left onto Main Street, and then another left onto Constitution Way toward The Brass Monkey. He got out and felt the sting of hailstones, then reached back into his car, grabbed a notebook, and placed it over his head. It was then he discovered there were no hailstones on the pavement. He reached his hand out, and again felt the stinging sensation, but he couldn't see anything. He had observed all sorts of weather conditions before, but this was new – a truly strange phenomenon.

* * *

Opening the door to The Brass Monkey, Ryan turned around and noticed the cloud moving back toward Long Island Sound. Then the sun broke through, for a moment, before disappearing, and a dark night descended. The moon seemed to have vanished into the belly of a black hole.

He walked into the bar, and discovered it was empty, except for the bartender. Ryan wanted to first make contact with Jack, who owned the title to the property and then, if he wasn't in, with his wife. So, he asked the bartender for Jack Zawadski.

"He's not here; would you like to speak with his wife?"

"That would be great, thank you." Ryan said. He figured he better get the ball rolling, and hoped Zawadski's wife could help somehow.

With that, the bartender went to a side door, by the cigarette machine, and walked out.

Ryan waited against the bar, for several minutes, when a women's voice called to him.

"Hello again."

Ryan turned, and felt blood rush through his body as if he were shot. His face flushed and his heart raced. It was the women he had slept with last night.

By the way she stopped walking mid-step, Ryan could tell she was surprised, too. Instinctively he knew, by the sly smile on her face, that their fling could mean trouble negotiating a deal. She would try to use it to her advantage.

She walked over, grabbed his hand, and whispered into his ear. "Let's go upstairs, and talk business."

Chapter 13

"There is never total darkness. Even in the blackest of holes, Light is always present." Translated from The Book of Lost Prophets*, Circa 650 A.D.*

Ryan knew the ramifications of what had just happened, his liaison with Jack Zawadski's wife, Sharma, was a detriment to the objectives of his job, and he had to stop it. He needed to put his foot down, and tell her "enough."

She wanted one million dollars for her property; within budget, but not within the parameters Tony had set. At one million there would be no money left for a company bonus, and Ryan's worth to the agency would be measured by the difference.

Sharma reminded Ryan, in bed, that the deal would fall through without The Brass Monkey, and she posed the hypothetical, “What if my husband were to find out?”

Ryan thought about the situation as he drove to the nine o’clock alderman’s meeting, to assess the local resistance group, called P.R.I.D.E., and their fight against TR Industries.

Ryan didn’t take Sharma at her word. If she stirred trouble by telling her husband about their sexual relations, Sharma was the one guaranteed to lose.

For sure, her husband, her standing in the town, and the money from the buyout, would all be in jeopardy. But, Ryan couldn’t judge whether she was crazy enough to do such a thing, like tell her husband, or how he would react.

“Maybe Jack was the insanely jealous type, or maybe he stopped caring, like Deidre and I did years ago. Who’s to know?”

Just the same, Ryan knew he had opened a door to a dark place. A place, just two days ago, he had shut and sworn off. He had intended to start life fresh. He wanted to drink less, and maybe find a relationship with a woman that was not purely sexual, but he found himself in the same pattern.

No longer was he invigorated by being with a strange woman, feeling the warmth of another body against his own.

Furthermore, the slight variations in scent, from one female to the next, were no longer so intoxicating to him.

In bed, Ryan went through the mechanics of love, but he was devoid of any real emotion, other than the base animal pleasure of being able to ejaculate.

"What is it with women? Why do I want them so badly? Maybe it's an ego thing? Maybe it is some sick conquest trip? Maybe there is some hidden dark motive deep inside my subconscious that makes me want them? How did I, the son of Bill Walsh, become like this? What's it all about?"

* * *

TR Industries was located in Houston and that was the name on the paper invoice, but they were just a holding company incorporated off shore. TR was not made of brick and mortar like the businesses that Valley residents were used to seeing and touching. TR was just a sheet of paper on file in the district courthouse of George Town in the Cayman Islands.

TR was one of forty thousand companies registered in the Caymans: a country that had forty four thousand residents, but bank holdings worth 500 billion dollars. The British created the Cayman Islands to shelter companies from paying taxes, and TR was one such company in a long line of tax evaders.

Ryan's commission, from past jobs, was wired from the Caymans, to Malta, to another company in Cape Town, which held the money for six months, to an import broker in Miami, to the Patriot Bank in Vermillion, Ohio. The same people who "washed" his money, handled drug dealers, and weapon smuggler's currency as well. Everyone involved took a cut, even the governments that processed the transactions.

The plant TR wanted to build in Derby was just the opposite, it was very physical. It depended on a 200-foot stack to dissipate the burn off of carcinogens into the atmosphere. And the plant would be visited by a caravan of garbage trucks daily in order to keep the furnace cooking. Ryan figured even if the plant caused no ill affects from the burn off, that the structural havoc the trucks would cause the roads, and the exhaust fumes emitted from them, was bad nonetheless.

Ryan knew this, and he also knew the property value of all the homes, which were counted on for retirement, would be greatly reduced. But Ryan also knew the plant would create lower taxes. That was the hook. The sell point. The soul sell.

Ryan arrived at 9:15 p.m. for the alderman's meeting at City Hall and it had just started. The chamber room was packed, so he stayed in the hallway with about thirty other people and watched from there resting against a wall.

Inside, McHugh, the Mayor, called the meeting to order by asking everyone to stand and say the Pledge of Allegiance. He sat in the middle of a long oak desk and was flanked by three aldermen to his right and three to his left. There was a fourth chair to his right, which was empty. Joe Romanzo was not at the meeting. Ryan knew the three aldermen to McHugh's right, because they supported the trash plant and were all paid, smaller amounts, prior to his visit.

Mike DeMayo coached the middle school baseball team, and his son was involved in numerous AAU travel teams.

Carol Jacobson was a divorced mother of four, formally from wealthy Westbrock, Connecticut.

Alex Brickle was laid off from a foreman's position at Sikorsky Aircraft.

Seated by herself, to the far left, was the secretary Ryan had met at McHugh's office earlier.

The meeting went into the first line of business, which was the public portion. Ryan watched and listened as different people took turns walking to the podium to speak whatever was on their mind. To a person, the only issue addressed was the TR Trash to Energy plant.

From old men with flannel shirts and blue jean pants, to high school students, and young mothers and fathers, they all spoke in opposition to the plant. Although Ryan knew the majority of the residents wanted the plant for lower taxes, no one was there to support the trash plant.

One man went to the podium, stated his name and said, "I am against this garbage plant."

Another man stood up and gave a long dissertation about his family roots in the Valley, forgetting to mention if he was for or against the trash plant. Regardless, everyone politely clapped when he sat down.

These were also members of People Really Interested In Derby's Excellence, P.R.I.D.E. And for the next hour members took turns speaking against the plant in often emotional and half thought out ideas. Ryan determined that the group was passionate, but not organized enough to defeat him.

Finally, the last person to address the aldermen was a woman in her late thirties or early forties by Ryan's guess. She stood up and, in a very dignified manner, walked to the podium. Her hair was dark, shoulder length, and full of think waves. To Ryan, she appeared to have come in from a storm, and the white Irish knit sweater and blue jeans she wore, added to the outdoors image he found so attractive.

She stood about 5'3" tall, but her persona belied her stature and she gave off an aura Ryan couldn't help but respect. She stated her name as Antonella DeLucia, and she addressed the aldermen with a very quiet voice and no hint of scorn.

Ryan listened as she first congratulated the aldermen for their dedication to the city, and how they had to make a courageous decision one way or the other regarding the trash plant. She told them that she knew in her heart that they would only do what they felt was best for the city.

After that, she gave her vision of what O'Sullivan Island could become. She compared it to Captain's Cove in Bridgeport, and talked about the benefits of building a marina in Derby, too. She mentioned the possibility of having a Naval Destroyer docked there to connect Derby now, with her glory of the past.

She talked about the advantages such a museum would have for the school children, and the amount of civic pride that it would generate. She acknowledged the benefits having a revenue generating plant would be to the city, but she questioned the possible health risks it might develop as well.

Ryan was attentive to Antonella as she talked about a river walk along the city, and he watched as she thanked the aldermen for listening to her, then turned, and walked back to her seat.

He noticed her hair bounce on her shoulders, and he stared at her hips as they lightly swayed from left to right and back. Then, as people applauded her vision, her head tilted down.

When Antonella sat, the recess lighting above her, reflected off the top of her head, and her hair shone a stunning color of black. Suddenly, as if an alarm was set to wake him from his trance, he noticed Tugboat Dan to her left, an obvious ally, and someone else he had not seen since childhood, to her right.

Dressed in a black suit and a Roman collar was Father Sheehan. He was older now, but there was no mistaking him, or his six foot nine inch frame.

Ryan left the hallway, walked down the steps to the lobby, and went to his car. He drove over the Hull Bridge toward his hotel, when the cell phone rang. It was Sharma, and she was waiting for him at the hotel bar.

Chapter 14

"Who will feed me? What if I lose my livelihood? Where should I go to escape danger? Why do I have this illness? Care not about yourself. Only in responding to the needs of others, will these worries disappear. Translated from The Book of Lost Prophets, *Circa, 1776 A.D.*

Ryan woke early and his hands were shaking. Sharma and he drank three bottles of Merlot, and his body revolted from dehydration. They talked about the P.R.I.D.E. group, and how naïve their cause was in believing they could halt forward progress. Ryan recalled that Sharma left at four in the morning, because he turned and saw her naked outline next to the glow of the alarm clock, as she got dressed.

Jack was returning from his business trip late that afternoon, and she told him that Ryan had visited The Brass Monkey to make him an offer.

Ryan proposed $400 thousand to Sharma last night, reminding her that the property was assessed at $250 thousand, and could be taken by right of eminent domain for much less.

She said nothing until his last thrust into her, and then whispered, “It’s worth one million.”

Today Ryan had trouble concentrating, and considered Sharma might be so stubborn as to sabotage the deal for her million dollars. He ordered black coffee and a side of bacon from room service, showered, and decided to go to Saint Mary’s Rectory and see Father Sheehan.

He now worried about the business deal for the first time since his arrival, and he figured the visit might do him good.

“Of all the women I could have met, why did I have to meet her?” He complained, “But it’s better to be in bed with the devil you know how the saying goes…”

* * *

Ryan drove directly to Saint Mary of the Immaculate Conception Church on Elizabeth Street in Derby. He was aware of the pedestrians who walked past his car in the crosswalk, and of the different buildings, he had seen during his youth, but he was in a type of hypnotic zone and he felt exhausted. What started out as a sure-bet business transaction had now became an effort, and he sought comfortable ground from his childhood.

Saint Mary's Parish, as it is known, was predominantly an Irish and Italian parish in the 1960's. It was thriving. And in an area where Catholics made up the majority, Saint Mary's was the mother church. Constructed of brick in gothic style, the steeple easily went 200 feet high, and had large stained glass windows, which depicted the life of Jesus.

To the right of the church was the convent, where thirteen Sisters of Mercy, along with several lay teachers, educated 900 students. Ryan remembered he wasn't the best student in grammar school, but he always found a way to pass to the next grade. When a crucial test was to be taken, his father would give him a pep talk.

"Ryan, let's pray to the Holy Spirit for enlightenment on your test tomorrow."

On the days when he flunked a quiz, his pitch was, "Ryan, let's pray that you pass to the next grade."

And so it went…

Ryan recalled the prayers always worked, or at least he couldn't refute the outcome, because he never repeated a grade. Regardless, in the early years, school was difficult for Ryan. No matter how hard he tried, the lessons wouldn't stick and the sisters attempted all sorts of measures.

"Ryan, stand in front of the blackboard until you tell me what that word says…"

"Ryan, write this five-hundred times…"

To make matters worse, Ryan was always in a fight with a monster of a boy named Biagio.

He was a new student who had just arrived from Italy, and because he couldn't speak a word of English, used his fists to express himself. Because Ryan was the tallest boy in class, the other students solicited his help regarding Biagio.

"Ryan, Biagio is after me, can you help?" Al Cowan pleaded.

"Ryan, Biagio pulled my hair…" Debbie Testone complained.

"Ryan, Biagio took my baseball cards, and won't give them back," Another protested.

And so the days went…

Each time Ryan asked Biagio to stop, and each time Biagio would punch Ryan in the face. Forced to fight, Ryan held his own; but who really wants to fight? Months passed and punishments were handed out, but the fighting never ended. Recess, which was the one thing Ryan liked about school, became a daily dread.

The recess bell signaled that it was time to fight Biagio, and Ryan's stomach ached from fear. Soon the fights became a given, and the same students who enlisted his help, now instigated fights between them. Like gladiators in a coliseum, their confrontations were for the enjoyment of the other students. Ryan and Biagio were recess entertainment.

One of the McHughs, Tim, acted like a bookie.

"I have a Carl Yazstremski and a Bobby Murcer on Biagio today." He'd say.

"I'll cover that with two Joe Peppertone's and a Horace Clark on the Raven." Rico Lionetti shouted back.

The Raven became Ryan's schoolyard name, and his opponent was known as Biagio the Bloodhound.

All that changed in the fourth grade when a new minister arrived at the parish. The priest's name was Father Sheehan, and he was 6'9" tall. To the students he was freakish. Ryan considered him a direct descendent of Goliath. The Italian kids referred to him "Papa Gigantesco."

One day, Father happened to walk through the schoolyard, as Sister Lucille and Sister Roberta were breaking up yet another battle. He marched over and picked both Ryan and Biagio up by the nape of their necks, and brought them to Mother Superior's office. Mother Superior had had enough of their fighting, and screamed that both boys were a disgrace.

"Both of you are expelled!" She yelled.

By now Biagio had learned enough English to catch the jest of what she meant, and started to cry. Ryan was relieved, because he figured the fighting with Biagio would finally stop, until he realized he would have to attend the same public school with Biagio, and he cried as well.

Ryan recalled how Father Sheehan intervened, on their behalves, and took them under his guidance. That summer, Biagio and Ryan played basketball everyday, except Sunday, under Father's watch. The next year they made the 8th grade team, won the Valley Parochial league, advanced to the state championship and lost, at the buzzer, to a team from Waterbury.

Basketball gave Ryan and Biagio more confidence in school and they became friends. Biagio eventually moved back to Italy, married a woman from Palermo, became president of a clothing company in Milan, but still found time to attend Ryan and Deidre's wedding in Greenwich. The last time they saw each other was by chance at Kennedy Airport.

"Ryan, I really miss Saint Mary school." Biagio said.

"Not as much as me Biagio. Not as much as me."

* * *

Ryan walked up the granite steps, which led from the sidewalk on Elizabeth Street, past the shrine to Blessed Mother, to the wooden steps of the Rectory. There he heard people talking around back, and walked to the side of the porch to see Father Sheehan, Tugboat Dan, and Antonella.

Today she had on black pumps, white pants, and a black sweater. Her hair was tied in a bun and she held a book in her right arm. Tugboat Dan still had his white beard. They hugged Father, then got in their cars and drove away.

Father spun around, as if he knew Ryan was there the whole time, and said, "Ryan Walsh, how in hell are you?"

Ryan smiled and walked around back to greet Father. His face was fuller and his hair was white, but he looked great. Ryan gave him a hug and stared into his eyes. Unlike the vast majority of the Irish, Father Sheehan had brown eyes. A trait passed on from the Spanish Invasion of Ireland hundreds of years ago, and Ryan always found Father Sheehan's eyes reassuring and sympathetic.

"Come innn for tea, Ryyy-aan." Father said in his usual manner of elongating words, which reminded Ryan of how Bella Lugosi spoke portraying Count Dracula in the movies during his youth.

They sat at the kitchen table and Rose, the housekeeper, brought them two glasses of Dewar's blue. Ryan smiled at Father's idea of tea, and held his glass up.

"Cheers Father."

"God be with you Ryan." Father said, and then turned to Rose, who was an unattractive women in her fifties.

"Hey Rosie, who's better than you?"

Rose blushed and walked to the next room.

"So Ryan, has it been thirty years since I last saw you?"

Ryan didn't have to hesitate. He remembered Father left the parish in 1971 under a cloud of scandal. It was rumored he had had an affair several years earlier with a parishioner from Saint Joe's in Shelton, and the woman had a baby girl. When the truth finally broke, the Bishop hustled him away.

"Thirty five years Father."

Father's arms went upwards and his head tilted back.

"Jesus, Mary and Joseph, how old am I?" He laughed.

Ryan laughed too, "You're in the hiss-tory books Father."

Although Ryan said this playfully, he meant it. To him, Father Sheehan represented an entire era called the 60's. He was a Peace Activist, a Civil Rights Activist, the resident Exorcist priest for the Northeast, and he once went on a retreat to the Monastery of Gethsemane in Kentucky, where he meet the writer and poet, Thomas Merton.

Ryan's father thought that especially interesting, because he was an avid reader of Merton. In particular, Ryan remembered Merton's books like, *Conjectures of a Guilty Bystander* and *The Seven Story Mountain*, always lying around the coffee table.

More importantly to Ryan, Father Sheehan was his basketball coach. Before he became a priest, Father attended Holy Cross College in Worchester, and played ball with Tom

Heinsohn, but he blew his knee out. Once he even arranged for Bob Cousy to attend one of their practices to give a shooting clinic.

Ryan often told friends the story about the day Cousy visited. It was one of the few stories he recounted. He didn't know who Cousy was at the time, because he was retired from the Celtics, and was not on Ryan's hero-worshipping list. Which, for Ryan, included Bill Russell, Mickey Mantle, Muhammad Ali, Joe Namath, and Pistol Pete.

But after Cousy dropkicked the ball in from half court, and made fifty free throws in a row, ten facing the opposite basket, Ryan was able to grasp he was witnessing something special. Cousy became a hero, and was put on Ryan's list.

"Tell me Ryan, how has your life been?" Father asked.

"Father, I've done well for myself, but my private life is a positive mess."

"You and me both kid. What's up?" He asked.

Ryan told him about his marriage to Deidre, and their divorce. He didn't go into great detail about her, or about why he was back in Derby, except to say he was just passing through from North Carolina revisiting the past.

Father listened and then said, "Don't let failure define who you are Ryan, because you will fail your entire life."

Ryan and Father Sheehan talked for an hour about the year they lost the state basketball championship, at the buzzer, and how, if they had had the three-point line back then, they would have won the game.

Then Father told Ryan about the trash to energy plant, and how he and others organized a group to oppose it. One goal was to obtain Naval approval to bring a decommissioned battleship to Derby for use as a museum.

“We are having a meeting here tonight at seven, why don’t you attend Ryan?”

Ryan felt uncomfortable, “Well, maybe Father, I’ll have to see. Remember, I’m just passing through…”

“Sure enough Ryan, but this will free your mind of bad matters. It’s a call to social action son.” Father said with his right hand extended toward Ryan.

Ryan stood and extended his glass until it hit Father’s.

“To social action Father…”

Chapter 15

"The Desert Prophet said, "On a typical day you can see one mile, on a good day you can see two, if you remove the sand." Translated from The Book of Lost Prophets*, Circa 1832*

Antonella drove to Altimari's Little Italy to buy Panettone cake for the holidays, purchased a new set of espresso cups, and then drove home. She worried about Sharma, she worried about the trash plant, and she worried about the vision of a strange man, which visited her again in her sleep. She needed answers.

"What does it all mean? Who is the mystery man in my dreams? Why has Sharma changed? Just days ago we were laughing, but now she looks at me with hatred, and she complained too often that "riff raff" people were moving to town and dragging it down. Why was she so annoyed? And what about the plant? Is it wrong or is it good for the city? Do I really know?"

Antonella went to her second floor apartment, and put the bread on the table. Then she took the coffee set and put it in the pantry, next to another just like it. She laughed when she saw the other set, because Antonella knew that she had a bad habit of "pack ratting" things.

She had one closet full of items she collected over the years, of souvenirs she got on different trips. Mugs from Wildwood and Ocean City, a miniature Liberty Bell from Philadelphia, mementos like that, and even old books and dolls from tag sales. She had a tough time throwing these items out, because she always believed they would come to good use some day.

She walked over, fed her fish, and then thought about the affair Sharma had with a stranger the other night.

"Who am I to judge?" She thought.

She pictured in her head Sharma's description of the man during sex, and imagined herself lying in bed with him, too.

"Maybe I should have an affair? Maybe I'm just picky? Even if it is a sin, wouldn't God forgive? Don't I forgive Him for sins against me?"

But although the vision of herself in bed with Sharma's stranger was enticing, Antonella said to herself, "enough," and looked at her fish tank.

* * *

She thought back to her childhood, and how she had this very same aquarium, rainbow colored gravel and all. Back then she saved up her paper route money and first purchased the fishbowl. Then, for weeks, she'd walk down New Street, turn right onto Howe Avenue, and then walk about a half-mile downtown to the Tropical Emporium, next to the Fine Arts Theater, and purchase a goldfish. Mr. Kyle would put the fish into a clear plastic bag, tie a knot, then instruct her to hurry home, and let the fish loose into the tank.

On Saturdays, if her mother didn't have to work, they would often visit the Bradlees Shopping Center in Derby, where there was a Woolworth's store. Her mother would call it the Five and Dime, but it was Woolworth's, and besides selling clothes, toys, and general household items, they also sold hamsters, snakes, turtles, and fish.

Usually, while her mother went shopping, Antonella would spend her paper route tips on a hot fudge sundae. After eating the ice cream, she would pop a balloon to see how much she would have to pay for the treat.

Each balloon had a piece of paper inside with a number. If the paper said ten cents, Antonella subtracted that from one dollar, which was the price of the sundae, and paid ninety cents. The paper with one cent written on it gave you a free hot fudge sundae. When Antonella committed her paper route money to the fish tank, she said "enough" to this habit.

One of Antonella's friends, Barbara, had a fish, in her tank, with long red hairy tentacles. It was called a Betta and the fish was so beautiful Antonella wanted to buy one for her own fish tank, but it cost five dollars.

This meant she needed to save her tips, and she did. She read up on the fish and learned it was billed a "fighting fish," because if you put two of the same gender in the tank, they would fight until death. Antonella concluded that Betta fish were ferocious, and decided to only buy one. She couldn't tell one gender apart from the other, and she was not confident that the fish lady at Woolworth's could either.

It was the summer of '73 and Antonella was eleven years old when she and her mother got invited to a beach house in Milford, which Father Sheehan's family owned. Two other families were invited as well, but neither had girls and Antonella didn't really look forward to going for a few reasons.

First, by then her brother Bobby was six years old and Antonella instinctively knew that the salt air, although considered healthy, would cause him to cough even more in adapting to the change, and this meant more breathing treatments, which he disliked doing.

Secondly, she would need to train one of her friends, probably Tricia, to do her paper route, and this would take at least two weeks, because Tricia would need to learn each customer's favorite hiding place on money collection day.

Her last concern was that her fish needed to be fed, but the door to their apartment also had to be locked. They never locked the door, but being away a week made this precaution necessary. Which meant no one would be able to gain access to feed them.

* * *

Antonella shook more Tetra fish food into the tank, and watched as the fish swam to the top and devoured it.

"I have desires just like Sharma, how is suppressing them normal? Why shouldn't I go out, find a man, spread my legs, and move on? How could doing what is natural hurt anyone?"

* * *

She remembered that when it was time to go to Chestnut Beach, the key to the door had to be located. This meant lifting up books, picking up chair covers, pouring out the contents of vases, checking under rugs, looking behind picture frames and feeling inside countless pockets of clothes hanging inside the closet. Finally, when the key seemed all but lost, Antonella's mother ran to the refrigerator, lifted up a statue of the *Black Madonna,* holding the black baby Jesus, and found it.

After that, her mother practiced opening and locking the door several times, to make sure it worked. Antonella remembered the solution she arrived at, regarding her fish, was to pour the whole contents of food into the fish bowl, and hope they all had enough for the entire week. She was especially concerned about her goldfish, because they were delicate and seemed to die too often.

A week later Antonella arrived home sunburned and eager to see her fish. After her mother unlocked the door, on two tries, she ran to the tank and was delighted to see the water was crystal clear. When she poured the whole contents of the box of Tetra fish food into the tank, it had looked like a dust storm, so she anticipated seeing a few goldfish floating dead on top, adapting to the habitat change, but none were. Then it dawned on her that the water was so clean, because every morsel of food had been eaten.

When Antonella pressed her head against the glass, she discovered that her Betta fish was missing. Floating on the bottom of the rainbow gravel was long red hair. Antonella, although very young, knew exactly what had happened.

The goldfish, starving, ganged up on the lone Betta fish and ate it. Faced with the possibility of dying, they choose to eat another fish, not of their own species, and live. Mob rule prevailed, because there were no more Betta fish in the tank. There was no equilibrium. There was no balance.

* * *

Antonella thought now about what had occurred. Yes, in one sense the goldfish were an example of the "survival of the fittest" rule. In another sense, the goldfish were a product of their famished environment. But to Antonella, what happened was commonsense.

To her, these delicate goldfish, which behaved like flesh eating piranhas, acted in accordance with nature. They did what He intended them to do; they fought for their lives against death, and survived.

But her muse didn't suppress her questions to God; it only strengthened her objections.

"Again, how would I do wrong if I did what was natural?"

But as soon as she asked this, she felt something blow through her. Her head felt light, and she almost fainted. Then like manna from heaven, a glimpse of truth nourished her like Tetra food droppings did her peaceful goldfish.

"The earthly nature lives for the present, but the heavenly lives for eternity...the cosmos are still evolving, everyone has a destiny in the mystical..."

She picked up a pencil, but was dumbstruck to write down one word of the revelation.

Antonella decided to undress, shower, and get ready for her P.R.I.D.E. meeting later that night. Standing nude before the bathroom mirror, she brushed her hair, and thought again about her biological urges. Soon she recalled the heavenly knowledge that touched her. Abruptly, she put down her hairbrush, and ran to her notepad naked.

All the blinds were pulled, except for the one in back of the coffee table, where her pad was sitting. Ducking to her knees, she reached up, grabbed her pencil and pad, and attempted to write. But the words dissipated inside her pretty head. Determined not the squander the opportunity, she struggled to describe the revelation then wrote: I'M NOT A GOLDFISH.

Chapter 16

"Prayer is the oxygen cord to He who is life. Sever it and wander aimlessly, like an astronaut, Lost In Space." Translated from The Book of Lost Prophets, *Circa 1965 A.D.*

After resting back at the hotel, Ryan decided to change and attend the P.R.I.D.E. meeting at the Rectory. Although he felt dishonest in doing so, he could at least meet Antonella in a smaller and more intimate setting.

He dressed in a cotton button down shirt, pleated Polo chinos, brown Italian leather loafers with tassels, and a Ralph Lauren tweed blazer. As an accent, he uncharacteristically decorated himself with a Rolex watch. He wanted to make sure Antonella noticed him.

At the hotel bar, Ryan ordered a Scotch, and passed the next few minutes by observing twin brothers, who spoke a foreign language, play cards. Ryan couldn't determine which game they were playing, but it seemed to be a "drinking game." Both took turns flipping a card from the top of the pile, then laughed, and took a shot of Kentucky Bourbon.

The twin to the right said, "Good luck," in broken English repeatedly. So much so, that Ryan determined that "Good Luck" had to be the name of the card game. At one point, it seemed that they were laughing at him, but Ryan figured it was just his imagination, so he said nothing. But sure enough, when he paid his bill and started out the door, the twin to the right called over to him.

"Good luck," he said, and then swallowed a shot of bourbon.

Ryan smiled, said "Good luck," and then went to his car and drove north over the Isaac Hull bridge to Derby. He noticed that the dredging equipment was moved closer to O'Sullivan Island, then he exited at Seymour Avenue, turned right up East Ninth Street, then onto Olivia Street-Irish Main, past his old homestead, and thought about his father's book, *The Book of Lost Prophets*, as well as *Finnegan's Wake*, past his old school yard, then down to the back side of the rectory, where he parked his car, and walked inside the kitchen area.

"Ryan, welcome." Father Sheehan said.

Ryan nodded his head to Father and stood in front of the kitchen door.

"Everyone, this is an old altar boy and great outside hoop shooter, Ryan Walsh. He is just passing through, so I asked him to visit us."

Ryan waved his hand as he turned to greet everyone in the room. They in turn greeted him by waving their hands, or saying, "Welcome."

"Ryan grew up on Olivia Street, and is visiting from…" Father turned to Ryan for assistance, as he couldn't recall where Ryan was now living.

"Charlotte Father," Ryan said without hesitation.

"Charlotte," Father repeated, "after thirty some odd years. He was with me during the 60's. He's a good man, and we need all the opinions we can get for the cause."

Everyone smiled and looked at Ryan.

"Come sit down Ryan, sit," Father said.

Father motioned for Ryan to be seated near to him, but Ryan noticed an empty chair next to an old lady in front of him, and sat next to her. Accidentally he stepped on her overstuffed pocket book which was beneath the table. She pulled it closer to her with her left foot.

Immediately Ryan surveyed the room and found Antonella to the right of Father Sheehan. Tugboat Dan was not at the organization's meeting.

Antonella had on a white blouse, which accented her rosy cheeks. She looked his way. One side of her lip curled up and the other side bent down, the feature reminded him of someone he had seen before, but he couldn't place who that person was.

"Elvis." Ryan thought. To Ryan, Antonella had the same sensual smile Elvis Presley had that endeared him to so many.

The meeting started with a prayer, which was typical of grass roots organizations Ryan had observed across the country. Mobile, Jackson, Detroit, Timmonsville, Belle Glade, you name the city, and all the meetings were the same. They started with a prayer or reflection, before mumbling started, and then different members blurted out grandiose ideas about how to stop the trash to energy plant.

A Mr. Gonzales had gotten email addresses of many parents with grammar school kids through the high school, and would email them the time and date of the next alderman's meeting. Yarak Czejkowski wanted to take an advertisement out in *The Evening Sentinel* newspaper, but needed one-hundred dollars to have it printed.

Mrs. Santo added she would have a cookie sale to help defray the costs.

"I just need someone to go to Stop & Shop for the ingredients," she said.

Mr. Walters, who spoke with a distinguished Jamaican accent, mentioned the local cable access network would be a great way to educate the public on the issue.

A longhaired guy, with buckteeth, wanted everyone to wear dust masks to all the meetings. A heavy lady, who had just visited relatives in Atlanta, proposed contacting CNN to do a follow up piece to the one they did several years ago, when the young couple's home burnt down. The piece was called, "The Valley of Brotherly Love."

"Only this time, they can call it 'The Death Valley Days.' I met a lady in line at the Piggly Wiggly supermarket, outside Atlanta, whose son works at CNN, I'll call her…"

Ryan listened, but mostly observed Antonella as she took notes. She looked at everyone that spoke with direct eye contact. Even when multiple people were speaking to her, she instinctively knew when to turn away, and when to turn back.

Ryan hoped to make eye contact with her, but couldn't at first. Then the old lady he sat next to, Mrs. Duffy, reminded everyone that it was too late for all of these ideas and that a "prayer in" at O'Sullivan Island was more practical.

"We can have it on Monday, after nine o'clock mass," Mrs. Duffy proposed.

While Mrs. Duffy spoke, Antonella looked in her direction and, for a millisecond, her eyes drifted over and met Ryan's, then immediately they turned back to Mrs. Duffy.

Ryan felt something tug within him, and hoped it wasn't his imagination. He looked for signs that maybe feelings stirred in Antonella too, and he watched as she threw her hair back ever so slightly, and yawned. Then she covered her mouth with her left hand, and gently lowered it to her shirt, and pulled on it like she was uncomfortably warm. Her cheeks were rosier than before, and a pink rash appeared on her neck for the next half an hour.

Ryan was hoping to speak with Antonella; but the old lady he sat next to, Mrs. Duffy, got his ear.

She was about seventy and had piercing blue eyes, which reminded Ryan of Mother Superior from grade school. But what Ryan found more discerning, was that she had Rosary beads in her hand that she whipped around like nunchakus, and the crucifix, which fastened to it, came way too close to his face.

She told Ryan how her son Kurt was a daredevil, and almost killed himself skiing by going downhill racing on the fringe of the treed area. Unfortunately, he hit a rock and flew into a forested section, missing two maple trees by inches.

"It was a miracle my Kurt didn't die," she kissed her beads.

Mrs. Duffy mentioned that yesterday she attempted to cross the street to get to the mailbox, when her husband called to her from the window, and she stopped to answer him. At that instant, a car recklessly turned the corner.

"But through the grace of God I would be killed," she said, again kissing the black Rosary beads.

"Why, just last week, my husband fell from the second floor working on a ladder. Had we not cleaned out the basement the day before, there would not have been a mattress outside to break his fall."

Ryan listened to her politely, but really wanted to introduce himself to Antonella who stood next to Father Sheehan on the other side of the table. She occasionally glanced his way, so Ryan continued to listen to Mrs. Duffy like he was interested.

And he did find something interesting. He noticed that in all Mrs. Duffy's stories about miracles, she never once mentioned that she deserved such intervention. To the contrary, she questioned why she was so blessed.

"In my youth, I was no angel. I was considered a party girl."

"What a relief," Ryan thought, "to hear someone who didn't moan about why bad things happened to them. Just the opposite. She was questioning why good things always happened to her."

Ryan found her view of life curious. She wasn't bragging about how fortunate occurrences came her way; she was concerned about why she was so blessed. In fact, Mrs. Duffy hinted that she was not good enough of a person for God to always favor her.

She sounded perturbed. Like she thought God was playing a dark prank on her. Ryan knew people usually got angry with God when something went wrong, but he never met anyone who got angry with Him when everything went right.

Was Mrs. Duffy the first one? Was her luck attributed to the power of prayer and the rosary beads she held in her hand? Ryan's father always told him that prayer was vital to life, that humble prayer to God was more real than the monthly bills, and more important than food. Just the same, Ryan couldn't help but think that sweet Mrs. Duffy was just lucky.

"If prayer was so real, and Mrs. Duffy was truly mad for God helping her all the time, she should climb the steeple and jump." Ryan figured, "That way Mrs. Duffy could find out if she was the living proof of Devine Intervention, or if she had just been a statistical freak of nature."

But it didn't matter, because the social time was breaking up, and everyone started to head for home, in agreement they would meet next Monday on the island for a "prayer in." Antonella appeared to be headed to the front door, which meant Ryan wouldn't get a chance to meet her.

Luckily, Mrs. Duffy spoke up and asked Father to lead in prayer before they departed. Rosary beads flapping she spoke.

"Everyone let's hold hands, and give thanks to the Lord for all our good fortune."

With that, everyone gathered around the table and held hands. Ryan ended up holding Father's left hand and Mrs. Duffy's right. Antonella was holding Father's right hand. Then, when Mrs. Duffy asked everyone to bow their heads, Father, for no apparent reason, switched places with Ryan.

This meant Ryan was next to Antonella. She held out her hand to him, and put her fingers between Ryan's fingers and held tight.

Ryan at first tightened, and then loosened up. He felt calm. The warmth, the touch of her skin was unmistakable. The feel of her hand gave him a reassurance he had not felt since he was a young boy. Was this the hand of the little girl who held his on the train from Grand Central, when he was ten years old? When a little boy peed in his pants, was this the same hand that had compassion enough to get him through the shame?

For an instant, Ryan believed they were still on that train. As though, the ride had not stopped, but only took a long station change before resuming the journey.

"Did she feel it too? Was it really the same person, or just my mind going haywire wishing she was her? I can't tell. I'll look for a sign," he thought.

The prayers ended and Antonella walked to the front door and left. Ryan figured he just got his answer. She was not that little girl. He shook Father Sheehan's hand and wished him good luck with his cause, when he noticed a twinkle in his eye, like Father knew exactly what Ryan was thinking. Then Ryan turned to say goodbye to Mrs. Duffy, but she was gone.

Suddenly car brakes screeched, and everyone ran outside to investigate. There they found Mrs. Duffy pinned between a car, driven by a man named Della Rocco, and a parked vehicle.

"If not for my new pocketbook, my leg would have been crushed." Mrs. Duffy proclaimed.

Ryan was happy to see that she was fine. Again…

Chapter 17

"Wait in the field alone, and I will come. When you want to talk, don't shout for all to hear, whisper, and I will answer."
Translated from, The Book of Lost Prophets, *Circa: 275 A.D.*

The sexual urges Antonella felt, subsided the instant she reached the rectory. She was tired from the nightly distractions of her dreams, and wondered if she would ever fall to sleep soundly again.

Antonella was greeted by Father Sheehan, as she walked up the front stairs to the rectory. She had known him since childhood and trusted everything about Father.

When her mother died, he flew in from a vacation in Rome, he missed mass; but was there the very next day to comfort her. When Bobby died, he celebrated mass.

Antonella had heard all the rumors about Father growing up. He was a womanizer. He fathered an illegitimate child. She even heard that he was gay, but she paid no attention to any of the gossip.

"He's always been kind, I wish that he was my father."

* * *

Antonella took a deep breath and was concentrating on her notes from the last P.R.I.D.E. meeting, when the door opened and a strange man walked into the rectory.

"Is he in the wrong building? Is he a salesman? Is he some lawyer the diocesan sent down from Hartford? Who is this guy?" Antonella wondered.

She was caught off guard, but knew the man was new to town, because no one in Derby dressed like a Wall Street broker. But no sooner did she think this, did Father Sheehan set her mind straight. This stranger was a friend. And Antonella found the man very attractive. To her, he was good looking. She felt her heart beat flutter and her face blush, when she made eye contact with him.

* * *

Antonella was too nervous to stay and talk to the man after the meeting, so she slipped out front to leave. She saw Mrs. Duffy walking in the Rectory parking lot, and yelled "Bye" to her. Then Antonella got in her car and drove home.

She felt like a teenage schoolgirl, her fingertips and arms were tingly, and her head felt light. She liked Ryan Walsh. He seemed like a good guy, and he was handsome, too. He had brown hair, a long nose, a cleft chin, and oval blue eyes. It was almost as though Antonella had met him before, but she couldn't place where or when.

"He is the stranger from my dreams! Now I have a face, to go with the outline. Thank you, Lord, the dream you gave me was a good one. Thank you."

Antonella made up her mind she would meet Ryan Walsh tomorrow, but she couldn't figure out how.

"I'll talk to Father Sheehan," she decided. "He'll know what to do. He probably has Ryan's phone number."

In an instant, she questioned that move.

"I can't call him, that wouldn't be right. He'll think I'm desperate, or some floozy. A man like that wouldn't be caught dead with such a woman."

Antonella arrived home sweating from the barrage of questions she posed to herself, undressed, showered, and went to bed naked. Her body burned as if she had the fever, and clothes only made her more uncomfortable.

She was thinking about Ryan Walsh, when she went into a deep and peaceful sleep…

Chapter 18

"Superfluous words are for the educated, who keep them for their own purpose. That's why He speaks in simple parables that the learned can't horde. The saying, 'man's burden is lightened when he helps carry his neighbors load,' is lost on the learned." Translated from, The Book of Lost Prophets, *Circa 1 A.D.*

When he left the P.R.I.D.E. meeting, Ryan had a message from Sharma on his cell phone. She said that Jack would be in the hotel lounge at ten o'clock to see him about The Brass Monkey buyout. Ryan smiled. He was going to increase the offer to $500 thousand dollars.

"Let's put this whole thing to bed," he mumbled.

But his mind danced between his mission to secure the trash plant, and all the people he had met at the P.R.I.D.E. meeting. In particular, he found Antonella stunning.

"I blew my last assignment in San Antonio, because I was drunk. I can't afford to have a woman's beauty intoxicate me, too. I have to be strong. I have to stay focused. After I close the deal with Jack, I'll end my fling with Sharma, too. Tonight everything comes to a close."

Ryan turned left out of the rectory parking lot, drove down Irish Main, over the Derby-Shelton Bridge, past the old Star Pin building, turned left at the light onto Howe Avenue in Shelton, past Downtown Danny O's, and then right onto Center Street and Bridgeport Avenue, toward the Marriott for his meeting with Jack Zawadski.

Because of his playing days in the NFL, Jack was someone he actually revered in childhood. How strange Ryan felt that he was sharing his wife.

* * *

It was 1969, Ryan was 12 years old and in the sixth grade. His late Friday afternoons were spent playing basketball at the Community Center, then watching *The Brady Bunch*, *Mr. Deeds Goes To Town,* and *Here Come The Brides* on television, when he arrived home. He couldn't recall if *The Brady Bunch* came before or after *Mr. Deeds*, but he did know he was a big fan of that lineup. Looking back, Ryan smiled. Whatever the local ABC affiliate had on, he watched. Ryan and Bill only received one station, and ABC was it.

A few years later cable was introduced, but prior to that they never got good reception, except for the local Channel 8, and they tried everything within Bill's budget.

First, different styles of rabbit ear antenna were used. Then a futuristic one, shaped like an inside out umbrella was fastened along the side of the house, but it kept loosening and banged the window during storms. Finally, his father had enough of the chaos and broke down and hired an installation guy, named Cox, who metal strapped a colossal sized antenna on the brick chimney.

After this measure, the antenna was so large; Ryan wondered how the house would support it. None of the neighbors complained, but on more than one occasion, Ryan observed motorists who passed the house and pointed at it.

In the end, all the maneuvering and expense was to no avail. Channel 8 was all Bill and Ryan could view on their television.

To their annoyance, every time a motor vehicle drove by the house, the television got static waves across the picture tube. The best they could hope for was that the tavern, up the street, had a slow night so fewer cars would go by.

1969 was memorable to Ryan for a few other reasons, too. He had purchased Mario Puzo's, *The Godfather,* and read a little each night, making sure his father never saw the book. Supposedly, it was mature reading and Ryan knew his father would have a problem with him having it, so he hid it from Bill like most boys hid *Playboy* magazines from their fathers.

1969 was also the year of the Jets and Broadway Joe Namath; Ryan loved reading about him in the sports section, and followed their weekly scores. In fact, Ryan couldn't get enough of football. He spent Monday afternoon reading newspapers and following all the teams, but he was especially interested in Broadway Joe and the Jets, after a Sunday game. But he had to visit the library to read about the teams, because *Monday Night Football* on ABC didn't start until the next fall season.

The Godfather, Joe Willy, and Friday night's television lineup aside, what especially made 1969 special to Ryan, was the local Derby High School football team. To him, what validated everything he read about the Jets, and made them real, was the Derby High team. In Ryan's mind, the Derby Red Raiders were the New York Jets.

During fall, after an enjoyable Friday night, Ryan anticipated the Derby High football games on Saturday mornings. The home games started at 10:00 a.m., so it was important to get there before 8:30 if he wanted a good viewing position.

Derby was the smallest school in the state, but had one of the best football teams for two decades. At every game there would be between 5,000 to 9,000 people in attendance. The town only had a population of 10,000; so having that many at a game was, for loss of a better word, insane.

The attendance was for good reason though; they were the best team in New England. They were also the largest team in Connecticut, and that included Yale and the University of Connecticut – the linemen for Derby High averaged 265 pounds. Hell, Ryan recalled a quarterback sneak usually amounted to a ten-yard gain!

They had a soccer style kicker from Ecuador, who routinely made forty-yard field goals. Another kicker never missed an extra point in three seasons. There was a big muscular black kid, who was utilized for kick offs and always pounded the ball out of the end zone. And they had a chubby white kid, who moved to town from Mississippi, and led the state in punting. In an era when most players had to perform multiple tasks, Derby had enough talent to specialize.

Most of the team members went on to play at D1 schools like Maryland, Wake Forest, Yale, Penn, Ohio State, and others.

To Ryan they were amazing to watch, and wearing a Derby shirt amounted to being a part of the family.

People from other cities looked at Derby residents with fear. It was as if the little mill town was incorporated as a gang. To an outsider, Derby was viewed as a modern day Sparta, and the assumption was that all that the people did in that town was eat, lift weights, and practice football – from the time they could walk – much like the residents in the city-state of Sparta prepared for war against their arch rival Athens.

* * *

Ryan laughed, as he drove past Simonite's cleaners, no one would be too far off in that belief.

* * *

The backdrop for the games was something a knowledgeable football fan would expect to see in places like Pittsburgh, or West Virginia. Derby was in a Valley, so the field was enclosed by hills – except the visitors' side. The bleachers only held 2,000, so the majority of the fans had to watch the game on a maple and oak treed slope.

From the visitor's vantage point, which was the one flat side, all people saw was a mass of fans, in red sweaters, standing on stone ledges, in trees, beneath rock shelters, and in the bleachers. It was intimidating.

* * *

Ryan called Tony from his cell, to give him an update on his assignment. He didn't answer, so Ryan left a message that he was on his way to meet Jack Zawadski.

* * *

Before the Derby football games, for dramatic effect, a man named Geno, dressed like an Indian, would ride down from the hillside on a horse, right before the playing of the National Anthem. As he descended, the student band hit the drums to imitate the Indian war call everyone is so familiar with in John Wayne movies, "Dodododoo dodododoo dodododoo…"

Ryan smiled as he remembered how well orchestrated the pageantry of the games was. To a twelve year old, it was magical. He loved the Jets, but he loved the Derby Red Raiders even more. And, they had just as much of a story line.

For instance, their coach was new to the Valley, and he was a giant of a man. His name was Lou DeFilippo and he actually played for the New York Giants in the forties. Big Lou, as he was known, played with Vince Lombardi during the "Seven Blocks of Granite" days at Fordham University, and he actually was an assistant with the Giants and the Colts of the NFL.

As big as the players were, Big Lou's size was even more prodigious. His playing weight during the NFL reached three hundred pounds, and that kind of girth is still big by today's standard. To Ryan, Big Lou was larger than life and so was the team. That's why he would never forget one game in particular against another valley rival, Seymour. The game was toward the end of the season, and both teams were undefeated.

Ryan walked to the field with a couple of kids from his class, Biagio and Lucky Palmieri. They called him Lucky because his sister was so good looking. To Lucky she was a bitch, but to Ryan and all the other boys, she was, well, sexy. Anyhow, they got to the game and drifted apart. For Ryan this was not unexpected, because the game meant everything and getting the best possible view was all that mattered, not who you stood or sat with during the contest.

* * *

Ryan "fast forwarded" in his head to the important things that occurred during that 1969 game, Seymour could do no wrong, and led at halftime 18 to 0.

* * *

"No worries. Big Lou will give his half time pep talk and the team will clobber Seymour in the second half," Ryan consoled himself, holding onto a tree from the hillside.

Then, after the third quarter, the score remained Seymour 18 and Derby 0. That's when, as if an earthquake struck without warning, the foundation to Ryan's football universe came crashing down.

"How could this happen? How could Seymour beat them?" Ryan complained.

Then, the worst possible betrayal shot out from Ryan's mouth, as he kicked an empty beer can in front of him, "Derby stinks!"

Ryan decided to walk the mile or so home and read the rest of *The Godfather*, but it wasn't to happen. As he approached his house, Ryan's father yelled to him from the upstairs window.

"Ryan, why are you back home from the game?" Bill asked.

His father didn't follow sports and had no understanding why Ryan loved football, so it was strange to Ryan that his father even questioned him.

"Dad, Derby is losing 18 to nothin," he said.

Ryan figured his explanation was self explanatory, but he was wrong. In fact, not only did Bill listen to the game on WADS AM, but he was furious with Ryan for not staying until the end.

"Are you a quitter?" He yelled. And Bill rarely raised his voice, "because I won't live with a quitter. If you don't turn around and go back to that game, don't come home. Now is when your team needs you the most."

Ryan was shocked and felt ashamed. He turned and ran back to the field to support his team win or lose…

And they won. Derby came back to score 22 points in the fourth quarter and win 22-18.

Ryan's football world was intact. But even if they hadn't won, Ryan was prepared to face his fears straight on and not quit, because of Bill.

* * *

It was with this type of reverence for football, that Ryan headed to the hotel lobby to meet Jack Zawadski. Jack played thirteen years in the NFL. First, with the Detroit Lions, next with the Atlanta Falcons, and then with the St. Louis Cardinals.

Back when Jack played, linemen didn't make an awful amount of money, but he was frugal and socked enough away to buy The Brass Monkey, plus he received an annual pension worth 55k. So, Jack lived comfortable with Sharma.

Ryan had a trading card of Jack growing up, and he felt guilty about meeting him because of his affair with Sharma. He was a celebrity of sorts to Ryan. He read about Jack in the Monday newspapers, and occasionally saw him on television during the late 1970's.

"If he knows about Sharma, I'm a dead man," Ryan worried.

He got out of his car, went into the lobby, past the front desk, and into the lounge, where he spotted 6'7" Jack Zawadski.

"Jack Zawadski?" Ryan asked.

He turned, "Yes."

"I'm Ryan Walsh," he said, and extended his hand.

Jack shook Ryan's hand. Ryan noticed his fingers were twisted, and seemed cold. Then, looking at his enormous size, Ryan remembered his nickname "The Dancing Grizzly" from the back of his playing card. During Jack's football career, he had a beard and curly hair; which, along with his height, only added to the bear persona. Now he was clean-shaven.

Ryan sat and commented about the weather, then mentioned how he had been to The Brass Monkey and met his wife Sharma.

"I know," Jack said and took a sip of beer.

"Listen, how much do you know about the trash to energy plant?" Ryan started…

"Not much," Jack said looking around the bar as if he were expecting someone else; then, looking down asked, "Play any ball Ry?"

"No." Ryan said, but felt flattered that he asked.

"No? Then you must lift weights to stay in shape?"

"Not really." Ryan answered, and then started again about the trash plant, but Jack interrupted…

"I understand you are staying here, let's go to your room. I don't want to talk business here."

They got up to leave the lounge and Ryan noticed the twin brothers were still at a table playing cards. When they walked past them, the brother to the right hoisted a shot glass of bourbon and grinned.

"Good luck."

* * *

Ryan noticed that Jack walked with a limp to the elevator, which took them to the fourth floor and Ryan's room. Once inside, Jack settled his big framed body and bum leg on the corner of the bed.

Ryan started to tell Jack about the benefits of the trash plant. He told Jack that most people gave these plants bad reputations, but once they were built, the benefits were appreciated and that the plants were clean.

Jack listened, and repeated the same sentence over and over again, as Ryan rattled off a plethora of benefits the trash plant would provide.

"Derby will enlarge their tax base." Ryan said.

"Gotta have it."

"Derby will have favorable grant status with the Federal Government."

"Gotta have it."

"Derby will increase its job base."

"Gotta have it."

"Derby will have access to new infrastructure money."

"Gotta have it."

"You will be paid $500,000 for your property assessed at $250,000. A nice profit."

"Gotta have it."

At that point, Ryan expected a little more banter from Jack, but his reply was the same. Looking more closely, Ryan noticed his eyes seemed glazed over, like he wasn't even listening. Then the realization hit Ryan that Jack was staring at his waist.

"What Jack gotta have," he thought, "is me."

Ryan was nervous. He had never been in a situation like that before, and he felt vulnerable. The door was closed, and Jack was twice his size. To make matters worse, the heater was turned on high, which made the room stuffy, and the amount of Club Man after shave Jack wore was nauseating.

"If he wanted to, he could have his way with me," Ryan worried, stepping back from Big Jack.

Ryan was in a dilemma. How could he get out of this circumstance without offending Jack? Should he acknowledge his advance and tell him no? What should he do? He didn't want to blow the property deal, but what was the correct response?

Ryan reached for the contract, and put it, along with a pen, in front of Jack to sign.

"No, not now Ryan, we'll talk again."

With that said, Jack got up, left the room, and Ryan locked the door. He poured himself a drink, turned off the room heater and then sat on the couch.

He thought about Jack being gay. He thought about his job. He thought about Deidre and the young man who committed suicide. He thought about his drinking. He thought about Antonella. He thought about Joe Pickum. He thought about his adultery with Sharma. He thought about his father.

"We all have our crosses to bear Ryan, and the way we carry our cross, affects the weight of our neighbors. God's design for you, in the mystical, may not be the same as for me. Be patient, be humble, be understanding, but stay diligent in your quest to find God."

Fifteen minutes later, there was a knock on the door, and Ryan opened it. It was Sharma.

"C-c'mon in Sharma."

Chapter 19

"All are called, and contribute to the mystery of the new creation." Translated from, The Book of Lost Prophets. *Circa: 1955 A.D.*

It was a special sun filled day. It was an innocent day, a simple day, and Ryan, like everyone, needed one of those days to nourish his spirit, while he lay in bed.

The rays burst through the hotel's east side window, and heated his face the way it did many Saturday mornings during his childhood. For a minute, he felt like he was indeed six years old. It seemed he had time traveled through a planetary "wormhole" in space, and landed back in 1963. It was a so-called out of body experience, and Ryan was watching *Astro Boy* on television.

He saw the futuristic android fly over his city to maintain peace, while the show's theme song blared in the background.

Astro boy bombs away. On your mission today.

Hear the count down, and the blast off.

Go, go, go, Astro boy.

Ryan was in a magical state, where nothing was complicated. It was a place where all he had to do was roll out of bed, and watch cartoons. A place where everything was fun and surreal. A place where his biggest concern was having enough Captain Krunch or Life cereal to eat. The space zone he visited was a place where everything was good or bad. Johnny Quest was good. Ezekiel Rage was bad. Mighty Mouse was good. Oilcan Harry was bad. Underdog was good. Riff Raff was bad. Josie and the Pussycats were very, very good…

So, those were the friends he waved to, as he back peddled through time. And after he returned from the land of '63, which was the land of *Petticoat Junction*, *My Three Sons*, *The Beatles*, and the Kennedy Assassination, he heard the familiar sound of ESPN's *Sports Center*. Ryan half listened to the show, as he decompressed from that place Einstein, Godel and Hawkins could only attempt to visit in mathematical theory.

ESPN did a special about Magic Johnson, and his efforts in the NBA Championships during the 1979-80 season. That was the year Kareem Abdul-Jabbar had to sit out a game, and Magic played center for the first time since high school. Ryan was in graduate school when Magic had 42 points, fifteen rebounds, seven assists, three steals, and one blocked shot. In one of the most improbable wins in NBA history, he put his teammates on his back and carried them to victory over Dr. J and the 76ers.

* * *

Suddenly the phone rang, and pulled him the remainder of the way from his journey. It was Father Sheehan, and he wanted Ryan to do him a favor.

"Ryan, will you give Antonella a ride?" He asked.

"When?" Ryan answered surprised.

"Now." Father said.

"I'll be right over."

Ryan got out of bed, showered, changed and jogged to his car. The whole while, the reprise, "Go, go, go, Astro Boy," repeated in his head.

When he got to the rectory, Antonella and Father Sheehan were waiting for him in the kitchen.

"Well it's about time, where have you been?" she said.

But before Ryan could reply, Antonella answered her own question.

"You must have stopped to get Father and me some coffee."

"Well?" Father furthered the inquiry.

Antonella shook her head, "Father, you didn't tell me he had short arms and deep pockets. That's okay, Ryan, I wouldn't want you to sprain your wrist by reaching into your pocket, and buying an old priest and a damsel in distress a coffee. I need you to drive the car."

Ryan stood open mouthed and said, "What?"

Father and Antonella laughed.

"Ryan, we are just busting on you. Let's go," she said.

"Where are we going?" Ryan asked.

"Antonella is a Eucharistic Minister for the parish, and she needs to minister to several elderly people who can't attend mass," Father explained, "She has her hands full today, so I thought she could use some help, and seeing that you are on vacation Ryan, I figured you wouldn't mind."

"My pleasure Father," he said.

With that Antonella got up, reached for her coat, and headed to the door. She had on a UConn Women's basketball sweatshirt, blue jeans and Adidis sneakers. She reached out her hand, and thanked Ryan for his help.

"I truly appreciate it."

Her brown eyes were sincere and made Ryan feel important. They got into his car and first drove one block away to 50 Hawkins Street. There, Antonella reached into the bag she was carrying and pulled out a chalice. Then she reached into the bag again and took out a red floral fleece blanket. By the jagged edges, Ryan could tell the blanket was hand made.

"Ryan, would you like to come in with me?" She asked.

"I'll wait here Antonella," he said, uncomfortable with the thought of visiting an old, sick person he didn't even know.

Ryan watched as she walked into the building, while he sat in the car and listened to the radio waiting for her return. For twenty minutes he stared at the dashboard and remembered how his father always had a statue of Saint Christopher fastened there. His dad often donated to various charities and each order gave him different gifts to show their appreciation. Catholic Charities sent pictures of young children his age from Africa and Asia, and Ryan believed it when his father told him that they were his brothers and sisters. So much so, that in the second grade, he brought the pictures to school for "Show & Tell." The Franciscans sent the Saint Christopher statues, which were placed on the dashboard.

Saint Christopher was the patron Saint of Travel, and Ryan laughed when he recalled how he always confused him with the story of a troll who lived under a bridge extorting money from people who passed over it. That's because Saint Christopher was a large hermit, who lived in a shack by water, too. He put people on his back and carried them across a treacherous river, much like a human ferry.

Ryan felt light headed, like he was hallucinating, and imagined himself as a modern day Saint Christopher, because he was driving Antonella around town. Then his focus was on the sensation he experienced when he held her hand at the P.R.I.D.E. meeting last night.

"Was she that little girl at Grand Central or not? Maybe we knew each other in a previous life? Maybe we lived hundreds of years ago in some old Spanish village? Or maybe we were lovers on some island paradise in the Pacific? Maybe Spinoza was right? Maybe there is reincarnation? If minds like Hawkins, Godel and Einstein suggested the possibility of time travel, then maybe the numbers could work out to support reincarnation? And not by factoring bugs, snakes, and dogs in the life cycle, just humans. Who's to know?"

Ryan's mind wandered.

* * *

After several stops watching Antonella take the chalice, and a handmade blanket, to a different elderly person, they finished.

"Tell me something Antonella, how long have you known Father Sheehan?" He asked.

"One, two, three," she counted on her fingers, "forty years," she answered with her crocked smile.

"Forty years! Antonella you don't look forty years old."

"Thanks Ryan, you're a sweetie."

Turning her head toward the sidewalk, she shouted, "Stop!"

Ryan steered the car to the street curb, as Antonella rolled down her window.

"Hey Stephan, want a ride?" A thin man, with a protruding forehead, and bulging eyes, got into the car. Antonella introduced him to Ryan.

He was walking to his second job at a machine shop, where he operated a Bullard vertical turning lathe, repairing train wheel hubs for Metro North.

They drove to Ansonia, where Stephan was employed, then Antonella reached into her bag, "I almost forgot, Father asked that I give one of these to you."

She gave him a blanket, then a kiss on the cheek. Stephan thanked her for the gift, and Ryan for the ride. Then he walked into the factory.

Antonella explained that Stephan had immigrated to the states, because of the war in Yugoslavia. He worked two jobs and sent home most of his money to his family who was still struggling over in Europe.

"Hey, how about buying me lunch?" She asked.

"Just tell me where," Ryan said.

But before Antonella could answer, her cell phone rang. Although she was on vacation, three nurses called in sick at the hospital, and Antonella was needed to fill in.

"I'm a cheap date Ryan, you don't even have to pay for my lunch," she joked, her smile suddenly looking even more seductive to Ryan.

Ryan drove her to the rectory parking lot so she could get her car, and then headed back to his hotel.

Driving past the front of the church, he noticed a wedding party gathered on the granite steps. The car in front of him slowed to a stop, so Ryan glanced at the people congratulating the bride and groom.

In the reception line he noticed Nunzio, the guy he met at The Brass Monkey, shaking the groom's hand.

"Could it be Ann Marie forgave Ass Wipe about the stag party? Was Nunzio wrong?" Ryan couldn't tell.

"Maybe it was a different wedding, but then again, maybe Gianni has a new brother-in-law." Ryan thought.

Driving past Altimari's Little Italy, he reflected about Astro Boy, Magic Johnson, Antonella, Stephan, and Saint Christopher. Each had people depending on them. Astro Boy had his futuristic city, Magic Johnson had his teammates,

Antonella had the sick and elderly, Stephan had his relatives back home, and Saint Christopher had the weary travelers.

But the character Ryan thought most about, was the one he confused with Saint Christopher back in grammar school, the big ugly troll.

He was a selfish, unsightly, giant creature that bullied people to pay him something in return for safe passage across his bridge. He was so demonic looking, that he was too ashamed to come out from below the bridge, so he gave demands from underneath. In fact, his name was Troll Beneath.

Ryan remembered how the troll let a young girl, whose name was Missy, cross on the promise she'd pay him tomorrow. She kept her promise and continued to cross the bridge, giving something of her life to the Troll. A flower, food, and conversation were some of the simple gifts she offered. Eventually, the Troll Beneath fell in love with the girl.

Later, when Missy was in danger of dying, the Troll had to decide whether to come out from his comfort zone under the bridge and rescue her, or stay put and let her die. The Troll decided he had had enough of hiding because of his ghastly appearance, and he used his giant ability to rescue the little girl.

* * *

It wasn't much past noon, so Ryan decided to get back into bed and he tried to fall asleep. If for nothing more, he wanted to maintain the out of body feeling he had experienced all day so far. But as soon as he dozed off, there was a knock on the door. It was Sharma.

"What's wrong Sharma?"

She didn't respond.

Sharma walked in, sat on the edge of the bed, stared at herself in the mirror across the room and didn't say a word. Ryan could only guess at what was bothering her. He knew how she felt betrayed by the majority of the townspeople, who wanted her bar taken by right of imminent domain. He knew about the 10-1-89 tattoo on her breast, and how much she missed her father. And he knew she had not been intimate with Jack for some time.

Ryan felt sorry for her, but he really had no right to confide in her. It wasn't his obligation to tell her Jack was bisexual. Nor did he have the inclination to inform her. It was his job to secure their property, so that it didn't go through a lengthy lawsuit and delay construction, which would happen if the town proceeded with the process of imminent domain.

Then, abruptly, Sharma threw Ryan on the bed.

To Ryan, Sharma did not make love. She attacked you. She was in complete control, and she was fast and furious, the way he imagined a prizefighter like Maureen Shea would be between the sheets. Sharma was cut like a middleweight boxer, too. Her arms had more tone than most men's, and her legs were equally muscular. In bed, it was easy to see she had some pent up issues, to which, Ryan already knew the root.

An hour later Sharma rolled over and lit a cigarette.

"Jack left this morning for another business trip," she paused, "I think he finds me disgusting…"

Ryan said nothing, and watched her as she stared at the ceiling, her eyes filled with tears.

"All he does is travel and lift weights. I think he has a problem with his age. I think he is having a midlife crisis."

She took a puff of nicotine, and said, "He probably has some little hottie he is banging. Hey, maybe he has one of those erectile problems, but I wouldn't know…"

Ryan listened.

"I need to get out of this town, $600 thousand and you have a deal."

Ryan did not hesitate.

"Sharma, that would be fine, but the property is in Jack's name. He needs to sign."

She shook her head. "You suit types always think you know it all. You screwed up. He quick claimed sole ownership to me six months ago. Jack's not about money. He and I had a fight, and the next day he went to our lawyer and had it turned over to me. It probably just hasn't been posted yet on the city hall property files."

"Then why did you let me think I needed to speak with Jack?"

"I don't know… maybe out of respect to him. I still love him. I wanted him connected somehow." her eyes welled up and her head tilted down.

Ryan got out of bed and reached into his briefcase. He pulled out the contract, wrote in 600 thousand and then signed it. He showed Sharma where to sign, and she did.

"Ryan I'm really against the plant, but I have to move on…"

Ryan didn't say a word, he was relieved his job was completed, and he knew his sexual relationship with Sharma had just ended as well.

There was thirty seconds of silence.

"Ryan, did you ever stop to think the people of Derby will have tattoos on their hearts with your name on it?" She asked, pulling aside the blouse she had just put on, exposing the 10-1-89 faded blue tattoo on her breast.

Ryan had seen it before, and knew what she was implying. He turned away.

"You know what, Sharma? Did you ever stop to think those black tiles at Grand Central didn't get stained on their own? A lot of people contributed. A lot of people are guilty."

Sharma stared at Ryan, and a tear rolled down her cheek. She buttoned her shirt without looking down, and then felt for her keys on the bed stand, never turning her eyes from him.

Sharma left without replying; she forgot her copy of the contract on the bed.

Chapter 20

"The universe rejoices in the simple gifts of life." Translated from, The Book of Lost Prophets, *Circa: unknown.*

Ryan watched ESPN and had a glass of wine. He felt relieved that the deal with Sharma was consummated for only 600 thousand dollars, but he knew she would never be happy. She was in a bad place. She was all alone. But, having known her, he was confident she would make it on her own simply because she was so strong willed.

Ryan had called Tony and let him know the good news.

"I knew you wouldn't let me down," Tony had proclaimed, "you're a competitor!"

But Ryan didn't feel the euphoria, like he did in the past, from praise like that. The victory felt hollow and he figured it had to do with his admiration of Father Sheehan, his infatuation with Antonella, and his respect toward Tugboat Dan, for his efforts to get an old battleship docked in Derby.

There was something innocent and refreshing in each of them and he liked it, found it interesting. In a strange way, Ryan wished he hadn't gotten this assignment, that someone else had and failed. Yes, Ryan liked the benefits his job offered, and he wouldn't accept failure in himself for them; but, if he were not involved in the deal and had just observed, he'd root for P.R.I.D.E. He'd cheer for the underdog.

The hotel phone rang, and he hesitated to answer, thinking it would be Sharma or Tony, but to his delight, it was neither. The voice was Antonella's.

"Hi Ryan, I hope you don't mind me calling you, but I will be out of work in an hour and was wondering if you wanted to meet me for a beer?"

She stuttered when she said "you" and instead said "boo." Ryan could tell she was nervous.

"Hey, are you making fun of my stutter?" He teased, and then quickly followed with, "I would love to have a beer with you, Antonella"

"Great, I'll meet you at Downtown Danny O's at seven. Do you know where it is?" She asked.

"Yes, Antonella, I've passed it several times in the last few days. I know."

"Well, how about I pick you up at the hotel instead?" She said.

"Okay, see you at seven," he said laughing.

Ryan hung up the phone, showered, and went to the lounge to have a drink. He was shocked that Antonella called him, and he kept looking at the bar clock while he drank.

"Maybe I'll ask her if she ever went to New York as a child. Maybe she'll tell me that she remembered me, that she was the one who held my hand when I peed my pants. Hey, you never know. But then again, maybe not."

Ryan was also happy to see the twin brothers were not at the bar, and then thought more about his conversation with Tony. He had told him about Tugboat Dan, and his friend, who was dredging the river with the hope the Navy would award them with the battleship docked in Florida.

"That's the only wildcard I see, that can mess up the trash plant deal," Ryan had said.

But as the words came out his mouth, he felt like he had betrayed Tugboat Dan, and all the P.R.I.D.E. members.

For logical reasons, his allegiance was with his agency and their client; but his heart was with Tugboat Dan and Antonella.

"Don't worry about it Ryan, Senator Kelly is on the Naval Appropriations Committee, I'll call him. He'll knock it down," Tony said, "I guarantee there will be no battleship in Derby."

Ryan drank a Dewar's and came to one irrevocable conclusion, he wasn't happy. He felt alone. He looked at himself in the bar mirror, and contemplated his father's take on life.

"No man is an island, Ryan." This was his father's favorite quote. His father often quoted Merton, and then he sprinkled it with sentences of his own.

"We all need one another. We all complete one another. God communicates to us through each other."

Ryan didn't know if his thoughts had more to do with the Scotch or with some divine revelation; but at that moment he knew exactly what his father meant.

"The opposite is true, too," he concluded. "What good is all I have accomplished, if I can't share it with anyone?"

Ryan nodded his head, and chuckled. His father was a man of few words, but when he did speak, his message was clear, and it went straight to the core of a problem.

* * *

When Ryan was a freshman in high school, there was a city debate about the location of a large granite sundial at the library. It was donated by some philanthropist at the turn of this century, and although it was admired by most, some people complained its location was a nuisance.

It was situated on the sidewalk by the bottom stairs, and many townspeople wanted it located to the back of the library, where it would be out of the way. Some citizens, like Bill Walsh, wanted it to remain just where it was.

Finally, it came down to a vote, much like the vote regarding the TR Trash to Energy Plant, and Ryan's father attended. Out of curiosity, Ryan went and listened as one person after another got up to voice their opinion to the aldermen.

One guy said, "It is a gift, and it is not proper to move it."

An old lady told everyone, "I had my wedding pictures taken in front of the sundial."

A Mr. Larkin added, "Moving the stone might cause damage to it. It is very old."

Still another person complained, "Someone will hurt himself lifting that monstrosity."

Ryan observed that the aldermen noted all the objections, by writing them on notepads in front of them, but he could tell that none were being taken seriously. It seemed the complaints against moving it were silly, and Ryan figured the aldermen would vote for moving the sundial. To Ryan, the location was bad, and it should be moved, but he didn't voice his opinion to his father. He didn't want to hurt his feelings.

The last person to speak that night was his dad, and Ryan was apprehensive. He worried that his father might recite some mixed metaphor like, "You can lead a horse to water, but you can't make it dive for pearls," because he was given to such comparisons. Ryan was nervous that no one would understand his point, and that his father would appear foolish.

Most times Ryan knew what he meant, because he lived with him, but to someone who never heard Bill Walsh, Ryan was concerned he might seem eccentric. Ryan also observed that his father was not comfortable speaking in public and that his words might come out all jumbled and not make any sense at all to the other people.

Bill walked to the podium, blessing himself, and holding his hat in his left hand, thanked the Aldermen for their time. After fidgeting with his hat a little, he addressed them.

"There is no sun to the back of the library. If a sundial is to remain a sundial, it must have sunlight." He then walked back to his chair and sat.

The relocation of the sundial was voted down.

Back home Ryan asked how he came up with his words.

"I just prayed for enlightenment, and the Holy Spirit led me to that *Readers Digest*," he said pointing to the magazine on the table, "I read it in there."

* * *

His cell phone rang, and it was Antonella.

"Ryan, I'm sorry, but I can't pick you up…"

"That's okay, I'll meet you there," he said.

"I hope you're not mad?"

Ryan laughed, "Not a problem, I'll see you there."

It was ten minutes to seven, so Ryan paid his bill and walked to his car, when he noticed it had been vandalized – sort of.

All across the windows were peel and stick figures of Baby Jesus, the Wise Men, Santa Claus, and Rudolf. It was harmless, because they were not adhesives and easily came off. The figures were plastic and relied on water to adhere to the car window.

Ryan smiled. A person obviously mistook his car for someone else's. Strangely, he wished that the prank had purposely been done to him. He would consider the act a sign of friendship. A sort of acknowledgement.

Only when he got into his car, did Ryan notice that a plastic candy cane covered the radio antenna. He got out to remove it, and noticed a business card under the windshield wiper blade:

You've Been Klinged by the Kandy Kane Klingers.

Kling Unto Others As You Would Unto Yourself.

www.KandyKaneKlingers.com

* * *

On the way to meet Antonella at Danny O's he drove down Canal Street, past Salvo Asphalt, and looked out to the river. In the light of the moon, he could see the dredging equipment had been moved closer to O'Sullivan Island.

"They are gonna hate me if they find out I'm the reason the battleship won't be coming."

In his mind, he tried to picture a happy conclusion; but there were no words or gestures he could call up. These were not stupid people who could be fooled by a quick joke or flattery. They were not motivated by money. They were bonded by a mutual vision for their city. But why were they so militant against the trash plant? Why not just throw their hands up, say "enough," and submit themselves to the inevitable outcome?

To Ryan, the Valley was a small mill town area that resembled a rust belt type of city – like Detroit – but in miniature. Eventually the city would be infested with all the social agencies, drug dealers, pawn shops, and strip bars, typical of many older cities in the Northeast and Midwest, human dumping grounds for the poor and needy.

He regarded these places as a type of corral, where poor minority people were gathered into a defined geographic area, so the more privileged people, in the suburbs, would be safeguarded from dealing with their problems.

"Why can't they see it is a losing battle?" Ryan asked himself.

He parked and walked into the restaurant, which was in a turn of the century brick building. The right side was the older section, with an oak bar, and plank floorboards. To the left was a newer section with an open-air courtyard, where customers smoked. Behind the courtyard was another bar and Antonella sat there with a beer in her hand along with her friends.

She introduced Judy, Maureen, Dawn, Karen and Kim to Ryan, and then handed him a Budweiser. They listened to a couple guys, introduced as Mike and Bill, sing, "I Got You Babe," on the karaoke machine, before Antonella spoke.

"Ryan, how's that car of yours running?"

"Fine," he said, noticing her friends looking side-eyed at each other and smiling.

"No problems?" A sly expression accompanied her question.

"No, none I'm aware of-why?" Ryan asked, not telling if there was a motive behind her concern, or if she was just asking for the sake of small talk.

Antonella laughed and Ryan noticed two dimples appear on her cheeks. Her friends giggled and Antonella looked at them, and then turned back to Ryan.

"Hey, they're laughing at you," she said with her seductive smile, "let's get out of here."

Her friends laughed more, as Antonella slapped twenty dollars on the table.

"Let's go."

They left and got into his car when Ryan noticed Antonella was carrying a brown shopping bag.

"What, more blankets?" he asked.

Antonella laughed, then reached into her pants, pulled out her car keys, placed them on the dashboard, and then stuffed her hand again down her pocket, arching her back to reach further.

Ryan noticed the key chain, on the dashboard, had a prayer ring on it. The ring had ten beads to say the Rosary, and a cross on top with a birthstone imbedded in it. Ryan's father gave him one, identical to Antonella's, which he kept in his valuables drawer back home in Ohio.

"Oh, I need to lose some weight," she said groaning while she slipped her hand back out, "Hey here's my card."

Ryan took the card and burst out laughing:

You've Been Klinged by the Kandy Kane Klingers.

Kling Unto Others As You Would Unto Yourself.

www.KandyKaneKlingers.com

After a minute, Ryan asked, "Where do you want to go?"

Antonella looked at him with a shocked expression, "Klinging of course."

* * *

For the next two hours they drove around, sneaking up on people's homes and Klinged their cars and trucks. Antonella seemed to get pleasure putting the baby Jesus klings mostly on the trucks. It was Ryan's job to cover the antennas with the plastic candy cane, and place the Kandy Kane Klingers calling card, under the wiper blades.

On one stop, the victims had motion light detectors on their front porch, which lit, and they ran like kids to Ryan's car for a getaway. Another time, Ryan tripped and fell to the ground, taking Antonella down with him.

As they struggled to get up, Ryan could smell her body scent and his hormones kicked in; but he helped her up and they sprinted to the car laughing.

After they finished their last kling, they drove back to Danny O's and sat parked out front talking.

* * *

"Antonella, who gave you the prayer ring on your key chain? I noticed it earlier."

"My father," she said.

Ryan expected her to say more; but she hesitated, so he kept the conversation going further.

"Really, my father gave me one just like it."

Her eyes widened, "Is your father still alive?"

"No, he died thirty six years ago…" Ryan answered, remembering only that it was sunny the day his father gave the prayer ring to him.

"Oh, sorry," she said.

"No, don't be. I had a good life with him. How about your father, Antonella?"

"He passed, also." Her reply was guarded.

There was a slight pause, and then Ryan asked, "Did you have a good life with him?"

He didn't know whether to ask this or not. He understood, that just because he had a warm relationship with his father, didn't mean that Antonella had one with her father, too.

"Well," she said, "I never knew him. He passed when I was an infant. My mother gave it to me from him."

"I'm sorry." Ryan tensed up inside, knowing he shouldn't have pressed the question, and at the same time suppressing the impulse to tell Antonella he never knew his mother either.

"No, don't be, I had a stepfather who was a good man, but he died young- a construction accident. So is my mother. She died from cancer two years before my brother."

"Okay. I guess we are both going down a sad path," Ryan said laughing, intending to turn the conversation.

"Yeah, I guess we are," she chuckled.

"New subject. How come you spelled Kandy Kane Klingers with all K's on your card?"

"Now, that's interesting. Mr. Walters, who is a member of P.R.I.D.E., set up a web site to raise money for our cause by selling clings over the Internet. He came up with the idea. Mr. Walters is black, and he thought it would attract more people's interest if they saw KKK highlighted. You know, the curiosity factor and all…"

"What the…" Ryan was confused.

"Well, we let people post pictures of their Klinging on the site, and I guess he figured we would attract more hits that way."

"I still don't get it," Ryan said.

"Well, over a few glasses of wine it sounded like a great idea, but in hind sight it wasn't. But hey, we get a lot of hits, so it worked fine."

"Yeah, but did you get any Klingers posting in white hoods?" Ryan teased.

"Actually, if you count the couple from Boise who wore togas, yeah." She laughed, "Yes," she said nodding her head.

Antonella turned off the radio, which was on so low, Ryan didn't even detect it.

"So Ryan, how long are you here for?"

"Next Tuesday I have a flight back home."

"How about Christmas Ryan, where do you spend it?"

"At my friends home. He and his family are very close to me, and I usually spend it there."

"Oh," she said, "how long have you lived in Charlotte?"

"Listen, enough about me," Ryan said.

He looked at her and wanted to ask if she had ever been to Grand Central as a young girl, but was afraid she might say no.

"Antonella, I have to ask you, why are you so against the trash plant. I mean, I read about it, and it sounds like there are a lot of financial benefits?"

Antonella's body language changed as she explained to Ryan that her brother Bobby was inflicted with Cystic Fibrosis.

"Bobby had a hard time breathing until his death, and I know, no matter what scientific data they throw at us, it is a bad thing to have in a valley."

"I'm sorry Antonella. How old was your brother when he died?" Ryan asked, feeling both concern and embarrassment.

"He was only sixteen. But not to mislead you Ryan, he died in an automobile accident."

Ryan nodded his head. He saw the reason behind her fight against his trash plant. Then, he noticed a tear come down her left cheek, before she wiped it with the palm of her hand.

"Antonella, I'm truly sorry. I had no idea." His embarrassment grew to shame.

"Oh, don't mind me Ryan. I get teary eyed, every time I think of that little guy. And it's just that I feel somehow responsible for his death."

Ryan didn't say a word.

"You see, after my mother died, I had to support the both of us, and I was young. Father Sheehan helped out where he could, but we were poor. I was struggling to keep two jobs, when a tree limb fell on my car during a storm," she paused, "the insurance people were going to total it out. And because I owed more on the loan, than the car was worth, I couldn't afford to buy another car. I would have lost my jobs. Anyhow, a friend fixed it so that it wouldn't be totaled by not replacing one of the roll over supports on the top."

Ryan moved closer and slowly put his arm around her. She hadn't yet given him signs he could enter her personal space; but, he figured, not to show a physical sign of concern was cold and insulting.

"Then it wasn't your fault Antonella, it was his. He was negligent," he said.

"No. No. He had my permission. He was only trying to help. It wasn't his fault, if anyone is to blame it's me."

Antonella sat up, wiped her tears, and looked Ryan in the eyes, "I just figured, God needed another angel in heaven, so he decided to take my brother."

She bent over, kissed Ryan on the cheek, and thanked him for listening to her problems.

"I wish I could say or do something to help," he offered.

"You already have Ryan," she said, opening the door to the car, before turning back, "but if you wouldn't mind, there is a 9:30 mass for him at Saint Mary's tomorrow…"

"Count me there, Antonella."

* * *

Ryan drove back to the hotel, reflecting on all Antonella had told him. He thought about her motive to fight the trash plant, which was her brother who died from Cystic Fibrosis, and her mother who died from cancer. And he reflected on the void that she must have felt, having never known her father, because Ryan never felt one-hundred per cent whole either, having never known his mother.

He knew Antonella didn't let personal hardships make her heart hard, because of how she always tried to help people. And Ryan found that beautiful.

Before long, a connection was made to what his father had always said, "No man is an island," and Antonella.

* * *

Ryan visualized hugging her tight.

* * *

"No woman is an island either," he mumbled.

Chapter 21

"God did not create the universe, only to go on lunch break." Translated from, The Book of Lost Prophets*, Circa: 1941 A.D.*

Ryan slept well, but forgot about the mass for Antonella's brother until nine o'clock. So, he hurried to get changed, and made it to mass only five minutes late. He spotted Antonella, sat in the same pew, and noticed a slight smile when she saw him sit down. That smile was an important sign. He did not want to let her down.

He hadn't been to any church in thirty-five years, but the surroundings of Saint Mary's were so familiar that he felt comfortable as he looked around. He felt at ease. After all, Ryan had practically lived in this church during his youth.

He noticed that the Stations of the Cross were freshly painted to their original splendor. After Vatican II, there had been a push to de-emphasize the ornate. This meant glazing over the colorfully painted stations, which he'd always love to gaze upon, leaving them a ghostly shade of white.

Ryan never understood the reasoning, but in an effort to steer people to a more mystical idea of God, and a more ecumenical relationship with other Christian faiths, Vatican II gave the American Bishops and Cardinals looser reign to address their congregation's needs.

And since the Catholic laity was paranoid about their fondness of the two s's (saints and statues), the statues were glazed over too, and the large paintings in back of the altar, depicting the resurrection, had been covered up as well. Ryan could never understand the logic.

"It is a tenant of Christian faith that God became flesh, yet these clerics decided that earthly renderings of God were a hindrance to saving souls."

Anyhow, now all the paintings were revealed and the church was as he remembered it, over thirty-five years ago.

The pastor, Father Cirillo, offered mass, but Ryan paid no attention. To his amusement, Ryan noticed a person from his childhood seated on the other side of the center aisle.

* * *

Bart Berlotti lived on Tenth Street, which was only a few blocks from Olivia Street and Ryan's home. He was five years older than Ryan, and a great big guy. If he had to guess, Ryan would put Bart at 350 lbs.

Like everyone else, Bart had a nickname, in this case, "Babysteps." Ryan thought the alias was appropriate, because, let's face it, when a guy is that big, it takes all the gumption you can muster to walk, never mind walk quickly, and running was not a factor for consideration.

Babysteps Bart didn't mind that nickname, but he did get angry when some wise guy would call him "Fatso" or "Bart the Fart." Of course, whoever yelled these epithets was always a football field away. No one would dare yell such names to his massive face. Bart would have murdered you. On reflection though, it was as if Bart stored the insults and waited for the perfect opportunity for revenge.

Although five years older, Bart was a junior when Ryan was a freshman, because he held the Derby High record for repeating ninth grade three times. Maybe because of this, Ryan noticed he never hung around with any classmate in particular.

Most times, Bart never attended school, and sat at the local bowling alley with a group of older guys. Years later, Ryan saw Bart's name in the Hartford Courant for extortion charges, and the very same bowling alley he had always hung out at, was tied to the case.

Apparently, Bart was involved with some mobster by the name of Frank Piccolo, whose claim to fame was trying to extort money from Wayne Newton. Newton tried to buy the Aladdin Casino in Vegas, and was being strong-armed, so he asked for protection from the Gambino family.

Bart "Babysteps" Berlotti, from Derby, was assigned to help Newton by his capo, Piccolo. Later when Piccolo himself was alleged to have extorted money from Newton, NBC did a story on Newton's mob ties, and it caused a giant mess in the crime families back here in the East.

Piccolo had become too flamboyant for the mob's taste, and although he was a made man, people in the mob wanted him silenced. The Genovese family, in particular, wanted him dead. So, with the intention of keeping peace with the other families, Paul Castellano, who was the head of the Gambino family, allowed a hit on Piccolo. He was assassinated while in a phone booth in Bridgeport.

Ironically, a few years later, Castellano himself was gunned down on orders from John Gotti outside Spark's Steak House in

Manhattan. Well, one of the reasons for that hit was the Wayne Newton debacle and Castellano's handling of Piccolo.

Bart "Babysteps" Berlotti kept his nose clean and was spared. Bart never spoke to the media. Heck, Bart never spoke to anyone. It was rumored that Bart was the triggerman who had, in fact, killed his former boss, Piccolo.

* * *

Bart was a legend of sorts to Ryan, because of his toughness. One summer vacation Sean McHugh called Bart "Fat ass," when Bart walked past the Lincoln School yard. Of course, Sean then ducked out of Bart's sight behind the school, leaving Ryan standing alone in plain view. But Bart never glanced over toward Ryan, and kept on walking. It was as if Bart didn't want to waste one iota of energy in turning his head. It seemed as though all his resources were accounted for and turning his huge head would disrupt his equilibrium.

Ryan didn't run. He said nothing wrong. Just the same, he was somewhat worried that Babysteps might think he had been involved. Ryan didn't care about McHugh; to Ryan he was a jerk. But, he said a prayer to himself for protection. Because Ryan knew, it could be a day, a month, or a year, but Babysteps Bart would always get his man.

Like one of those giant moray eels that hides in crevices, waiting to strike, Bart would pounce on whoever mocked him at just the right moment. Never during normal school hours, because people would be around. No, Bart would wait for the perfect time when he could strike without holding back. And he had the memory to match his girth. Ryan knew, it didn't matter how much time had passed from the initial insult, Bart never forgot a barb.

After school one day, Sean, who was a kick ass kid himself, asked Ryan to walk home with him instead of taking the bus. He had gotten a detention, and didn't want to walk home alone. All the McHughs pissed off a lot of people, especially the Italian kids, and Sean was afraid of being jumped. Having Ryan with him helped, because Ryan never pissed off anyone.

Anyhow, after detention, Ryan went with Sean to get a coat from his locker downstairs. When they turned to walk away, Babysteps Bart was at the exit door. It was several months earlier when Sean had called Bart a "fat ass," but Bart hadn't forgotten. He charged Sean, and was on top of him in seconds. It was as though all his adrenaline was stored for that burst from the doorway to Sean, which was a span of about twenty yards.

Sean had a broken nose, a cut above his eye, and he laid in the fetal position, holding his belly. Ryan didn't think Bart was finished either. A knife fell out of his coat and onto the floor, but Ryan kicked it away.

Bart Baby stepped backwards.

He waddled down the hallway, picked up the knife, and then turned around. He looked Ryan's way, and nodded as if to say, "Good idea." Ryan nodded back, and then blessed himself, making sure neither McHugh nor Bart noticed.

* * *

Now, Ryan couldn't believe his eyes that Bart was in church, but he couldn't believe he was in church either. Sitting in the pew, Ryan couldn't recall a word of the mass, but he could recite what Bart and Antonella were wearing.

Bart had on black pants, black shoes, and a beige shirt that he wore over his pants to hide his stomach. A gold chain was around his neck, but tucked inside his shirt, and his hair was pulled back in a ponytail. Antonella had on black pants too, with high-heeled shoes and a red sweater. Diamond stud earrings and a gold chain with a crucifix rounded out her accessories. Her hair was in a tight bun.

Antonella leaned forward, and Ryan noticed her concentration. Father Cirillo introduced a guest priest he had known from a sabbatical in Rome. His name was Father Raniero Cantalamessa, and Ryan guessed his age was in the mid sixties range. He had a white beard, his hair was disheveled, and he spoke with a heavy Italian accent.

"God loves all of us," he said. Then there was a long pause.

"Even though we are all sinners. I sin every day," he added.

His sermon lasted the standard fifteen minutes, but to Ryan, it was powerful. He spoke about sin in a new way, and in a fresh way. He spoke about the need to educate ourselves about what sin is, and the need to fight sin, as well as the fact "we people" can defeat sin.

Ryan listened as he said all men and women can fail as husbands, as wives, as mothers, and fathers, as business people, and as priests and clergy, but that these failures were all relative, and that it didn't mean we had failed as God's people.

"Sin," he said, "is a failure to what one is, and not what one does. As long as man hides his sins, which only man knows through the Holy Spirit, it saddens him. As soon as we confess to God our sins, peace and happiness enters our hearts."

Ryan marveled at how simple he communicated a complex issue to the congregation.

"The fight takes a lifetime, and we must take steps each day, like a bambino, a baby, to repent and honor God."

Ryan numbed when he finished his talk.

"In the end, everything will be alright."

He left the altar and the church was in complete silence.

Ryan noticed the parish bulletin, to his left, had a short biography about him, and he read it.

Father Cantalamessa was on the International Theological Commission that represented all Christian faiths, and his personal ministry was preaching and writing books.

The last line of his bio sent chills through Ryan. Since 1980, Father Cantalamessa had been the preacher and confessor to the papal household. He was the priest to whom the Pope confessed his sins.

"Maybe, if my father were alive, he'd be reading his books? Maybe he was today's answer for the void left by Merton?" Ryan thought, tapping the bulletin against his palm.

* * *

Father Cirillo led the congregation in the profession of the faith, and Ryan stood up and recited it too. After the Holy Eucharist was consecrated, the remembrance of Robert DeLucia was read and Ryan glanced at Antonella and noticed she was crying. Two lines formed for communion, but Ryan stayed back.

He watched as Antonella, who is tiny, and Bart, who is huge, walked side by side up the center aisle to the altar. On the way back, Antonella was far ahead of him. This meant Bart "Babysteps" Berlotti was the last person down the aisle.

Father Cirillo paused uncomfortably long for Bart to take his seat, before proceeding with the mass. Ryan didn't think the image of Bart, walking back to his pew, was lost on anyone in church, including Father Cirillo.

The vision of Bart "Babysteps" Berlotti walking down the aisle, with his rubber-soled shoes squeaking on every slide, was not lost on Ryan.

Chapter 22

"All the birds in the air will sing, and the sun will shine forever when they feel His voice." Translated from, The Book of Lost Prophets. *Circa, 5 A.D.*

Ryan waited out front for Antonella while she greeted friends. When she approached Ryan, she gave him a hug, and Ryan was caught off guard and didn't hug back. A problem, he figured, because his unemotional response might be taken the wrong way by her and Ryan wanted to spend the day with Antonella, and build on their heart felt conversation from last night.

"Thanks for coming Ryan," she said.

She mentioned visiting her brother and mother's graves at Mount Saint Peter's Cemetery, and Ryan saw the opportunity to be with her and offered to drive. Ryan's parents were buried there as well, but he couldn't bring himself to drive past their plot, and was relieved to see Antonella's mother and brother were at opposite ends in the cemetery.

On the way back to Saint Mary's, Antonella confided in Ryan about Tugboat Dan, and his mission to get an old battleship anchored off O'Sullivan Island.

"It's called the Joseph Hull Project," she said.

Ryan knew all about Dan's plans, and felt terrible he had to squash the idea, but listening to the excitement in Antonella's voice, almost made him forgot that it wasn't going to happen, or that he was the culprit responsible for the project's demise.

She told him the story about Isaac Hull's father Joseph, and how he had led a group of men down the Housatonic River and captured a British ship, then sailed it back to Derby.

"Dan wants to imitate Joseph Hull and bring that battleship to Derby. He has friends in the Navy, and it looks like we will be awarded the ship. If it happens, and I'm sure it will, the trash plant will be defeated," she said. "People will realize there is another alternative to the trash plant."

"I hope it does, Antonella," Ryan said, while turning onto Elizabeth Street.

"Ryan can you drive me to the convalescent home?" She asked, "I have a friend who won't make it to the New Year, and I want to give her my first bread."

Ryan inquired what she meant, and she told him it was an Old Italian tradition her mother taught her, to give bread to friends on New Year's Day, as a blessing, and Antonella wanted to make sure her friend got her bread before she passed.

"Sure, Antonella."

She retrieved the bread from her car and they drove to the convalescent home.

While Ryan waited for her to return from visiting her friend, he thought about church and it triggered memories of Ryan's days serving as an altar boy for Father Sheehan.

* * *

He and Biagio were always scheduled for the 11:30 mass on Sundays. Then, after doing the little things like hanging up the cassocks, and extinguishing the candles, they would race home.

Biagio lived one street over on Hawkins, but they would use Ryan's home as the finish line. There was never any wager, just a friendly race. Most times, they pushed each other into hedges, or faked injuries, so that the other would come to their aid, only to run again and gain an edge. Then, after being "suckered," they ran the whole two blocks home laughing.

After arriving home, Ryan would sit on the couch and watch television for the next several hours. For some strange reason, both New York stations worked on Sunday, albeit in static. So Ryan would watch the *Bowery Boys* on Channel 5, then, during baseball season, the Yankees on Channel 11. His father always went to the seven o'clock mass, and then purchased cold cuts at Cappadagli's Market, before reading his books with Herb Alpert and the Tijuana Brass playing in the background.

Ryan and Bill each basked in their little island of peace.

Ryan missed those relaxing times, but today was close to the tranquility he experienced back then. His mind was not on women, or sales jobs, or booze, it was on simple things and spiritual matters, and he questioned his life more deeply.

Ryan recalled a passage he read from, *The Imitation of Christ.* "A passionate man sees good intentions and makes them evil."

"Ya know what," he thought, "I've been that passionate man. If a man did something good for me, I always figured, what's his angle. If a woman was nice to me, I just assumed she wanted to have sex."

Ryan thought back to the Greek philosophers and their views. "Didn't they believe youthful passions were a hindrance to spiritual development? Didn't monks and other religious, refrain from speaking, or did things like whip themselves, in an effort to atone for sins? Wasn't Father Cantalamessa's view of sin different? Didn't he imply, more or less, that sin was important for the glory of God? That sin was a fact of the human condition, and something to be conquered day by day?"

Antonella returned to the car, shut the door, and then turned to Ryan. "Let's go to Indian Well State Park."

Ryan knew the park, and smiled at the thought of visiting it with her. So, they drove down Roosevelt Drive, past Books by the Falls, across the Derby-Shelton Bridge, then onto Howe Avenue toward Indian Well in Shelton.

The State Park borders the Housatonic River and they inched along looking out over the water when they got stuck in traffic on Route 110. Then, just before the entrance to the park, Antonella noticed Ryan staring at a lawn sale in front of an old colonial farmhouse.

"Would you like to stop, Ryan?"

"No, just daydreaming," he said.

"About what? Tell me."

Ryan at first hesitated, but then told Antonella about his father's manuscript, *The Book of Lost Prophets*, and how he had given it away when he sold his house.

"If there is one thing I wish I had kept, that was it," he said.

Antonella could sense his disappointment; "Maybe one day you'll find it Ryan, if you look. Maybe I'll search with you," she said with her Elvis like smile.

"Thanks Antonella, I appreciate it."

* * *

For the next few minutes not a word was spoken, and Ryan thought back to the lost book, and how his father used to keep it in the middle of that glass door bookshelf that he had built. Ryan was never allowed to touch the manuscript, and his father read it late at night in private, except for Ryan's birthday.

Once a year, until he was about ten, a passage was read to him. "The gift of life is the greatest present of all..."

For some reason, that sentence stuck in Ryan's memory. And Ryan knew why. His father never broached the subject, but Ryan believed his mother died from complications as a result from giving birth to him. Her tombstone was marked one year later to the day of his birth. He had no proof of his theory, because he never investigated. To Ryan there was no reason to investigate his notion.

Just like a child knows it has the flu in its stomach, and can't do anything about it, Ryan just rode the feelings out and never asked. Ryan couldn't remember the rest of the saying, but he got the gist of his father's message in that one sentence. His mother died, so that he could live.

Now, not knowing the remainder of that passage from, *The Book of Lost Prophets* bothered him more than solid proof of how his mother died.

"Some things just don't require proof," he figured.

* * *

They parked in a dirt lot, enclosed by telephone poles laid out horizontal and knee high, used for fencing. They got out, shut the doors, and walked across the street. Ryan was very familiar with the park, having gone there with his friends during high school to jump into the well.

The walk to the well was like something out of a movie scene from *The Last Mohegan.* Pine trees formed a tunnel over a stream, and the dirt path, which led to it. The area was pristine, and sunlight barely shown through the density of the trees. The well itself was formed by a waterfall, which probably reached fifty feet high.

The falls was flanked on two sides by a rock formation that was naturally stepped to the top. Because it was stepped, it was easy to climb and jump into the water from different levels. Level one obviously was for the novice, while level ten attracted the daredevil. Ryan only had courage for level seven; he was always too scared to jump from the top.

* * *

Antonella told Ryan a story about a young Indian princess, from the Paugussett Nation, and a handsome prince, from the Pootatock tribe of the Mohegan Nation, who fell in love. It was a Romeo and Juliet type of story where they were forbidden to wed, and after also being banned from seeing each other, they agreed to secretly meet at the falls. On the day they were to meet, it was told to the princess, that her prince was to be wed to another woman from his tribe.

The princess still went to the falls, but when the young warrior prince was detained and arrived late, in a state of depression, she threw herself into the well making sure she hit the protruding rock at one side, which was dubbed "Dead Man's Chin." When the young warrior prince arrived, and discovered his young love dead in the falls, he too leaped to his death.

"They died jumping onto 'Dead Man's Chin,'" Antonella said pointing to the rock formation, "but their spirits lived together for eternity." She looked up to the sky as she said this, and Ryan found his head drifting up with hers.

"Listen, I'm not jumping," he joked shaking his head and putting both his hands up in a defensive posture.

Antonella laughed, and they walked further along the path, before it started to rain, and they ducked underneath another rock formation, to shelter themselves. Soon, Antonella took a stick and started to scratch the earth with it.

"What are you doing?" Ryan asked.

"Watch," she said and kept digging, holding the stick with both her small hands.

Finally, she held out her right hand, which was full of dirt, outside of the rock shelter to wash it with the rainwater. Little by little the dirt ran off her hand until an Indian arrowhead appeared.

"What the heck, Antonella?" Ryan said.

"Indians were hunter gatherers, Ryan," she explained, "they made arrowheads all day long. When it rained, they sat under shelters like this one, and sharpened new arrowheads for their shafts, and threw the used ones away. I have a whole collection of them."

Antonella took Ryan's hand, and put the arrowhead in it, then clasped it closed. She looked up at Ryan; her black hair was damp and wavy, and her brown eyes warm and inviting. To Ryan, she was perfect.

He put both his hands around the back of her head, pulled her close, and then kissed her. Antonella didn't resist. At first, her arms were limp by her side, but gradually they bent upwards until they reached Ryan's shoulder blades and locked.

They kissed under the rock shelter, by the side of the waterfall, for about ten minutes before it stopped raining.

Antonella broke away, stepped back three feet, and said, "Race to the car." Then she took off down the path. Ryan gave her a "head start" and then ran after her, being careful not to slip on the loose rocks along the way.

As he got closer, she tripped, fell to the ground, and held her ankle with both hands. Ryan got to her, bent down and helped her up by putting one arm around her waist and sliding her left arm around his neck.

"Is it broken?" He asked, stuttering.

"I'll be okay, Ryan," she reassured him, then broke free from his grip and limped about on the good foot.

"If you want, I'll carry you to the car Antonella…"

She insisted it was fine and kept limping around the path, while Ryan watched. Then, as if planned, she started sprinting to the parking lot.

"She 'suckered' me like Biagio would do," Ryan smiled.

Antonella was not hurt at all, and even jumped over the telephone pole fence to get to the car first.

She and Ryan laughed the whole way there.

Chapter 23

"Charity of spirit is on the top five gift list of all time." Translated from The Book of Lost Prophets*, Circa: 1912, A.D.*

When Ryan left Antonella back at her car, they made a date to meet for dinner at Fratelli's on Main Street. Antonella was full of excitement, and wanted to tell someone about her day, but she stayed calm in front of Ryan.

"Eight okay with you, Antonella?" Ryan asked.

"Eight sounds wonderful, Ryan," she said and then reached into her bag and pulled out a wrapped gift. It was dressed in red paper with a gold bow on top.

"I want you to have this for Christmas, on one condition."

"What's that?" Ryan asked, looking at the present.

"Please don't open it, until you leave Derby."

"I promise," he said, then took the gift and kissed her on the cheek. "This was very thoughtful of you."

* * *

Antonella got in her car and drove home. She climbed the stairs to her apartment and immediately fed her fish.

"I know I fed you already today, but I want to celebrate," she spoke to them as if they understood.

In her room, she sat on the end of her bed and smiled. "Thank you God. You answered my prayers."

She had all day to wait until dinner and she couldn't keep still. She wanted to share her news with someone, but didn't know if it was the wise thing to do, because it might seem boastful and conceited.

"I understand he is going back home, but I know we had a connection. I know he is the man I have been waiting for, all these years. Thank You."

She turned on the television, and then turned it off. She tried to prepare something to eat, but decided she wasn't hungry. She picked up a book she was reading, but closed it shut. She was giddy, and knew that when Ryan opened her Christmas present back home, he would return, or at least call.

"Sharma, I'll see Sharma. I know she is upset with me, but maybe my good news will snap her out of her depression. Then again, maybe I am just thinking of myself. Maybe I should just visit her to find out how she's doing and cheer her up. That's the right thing to do. But, if the timing is right, I'll share my good news with her. I'm sure she would want to hear. After all, she is my friend."

* * *

For the last two nights Sharma tended bar, then took a bottle of wine and went up to the widow's walk. There she sat, smoked her cigarettes, and drank. She looked out over the river and thought about the past week.

Where was Jack? Why didn't he call? Why did she even care? She couldn't decide what to do. Yes, she got a handsome sum of money for her business, but why wasn't she happy? Her stomach felt nervous, like she had to vomit, but she knew she wasn't ill. Suddenly, the madness she felt toward everyone in town didn't motivate her any more. Sharma felt alone, like she didn't have a friend in the world.

"Do I really want to buy a big house in the suburbs? Who would I know?"

An ash from her cigarette fell onto her blouse, and she stood up to brush it off. Unfastening the top two buttons, she swiped her bra with her hand, exposing the 10-1-89 tattoo on her breast.

The sight of it, which in the past proudly reminded Sharma of her father, now caused her to remember Ryan Walsh. In particular, Sharma recalled the last words he had said to her the other day, after they had had sex.

"You know what Sharma? Did you ever stop to think that those black tiles at Grand Central didn't get stained on their own? A lot of people contributed. A lot of people are guilty."

His words echoed in her head, much like a spear through her heart, piercing and deadly accurate. To Sharma, his words were also Prophetic.

She started to sweat.

"He's right. I sold out. Dad forgive me, I sold out to the suits," she cried.

She sat in the chair and started to shake.

"Help me God, I can't take it. Please help me."

Sharma wanted direction, answers, something to happen that would make sense to her, but there was no one to talk to. She had betrayed her best friend, and a lot of people in town. She needed meaning out of her situation, but there was no one to turn to. Sharma knew she couldn't face her friends once it became known she had sold The Brass Monkey.

"I have everything, and yet I have nothing."

The seven o'clock train whistle sounded and Sharma watched as it approached. She extinguished the lantern she had lit, and watched in darkness as the train went past.

"Sharma, are you up there?" A voice asked from the stairway.

She got up and yelled downstairs, "Yeah, who is it?"

"It's me, Nell. Where have you been? I'm worried about you," she said.

Sharma took a deep breath, "I'll be right there, I need to talk to you," her words cracked in her throat.

She got up, and walked down the stairs to embrace Antonella. Her body jerked, and her nose ran, as she tried to speak.

"I'm sorry. I'm sorry."

Antonella patted her back with one hand, and stroked her blonde hair with the other.

"Don't worry, everything will be alright. Everything will be alright, Sharma." Antonella didn't know why Sharma was so upset, but guessed it had to do with her husband Jack.

"It's just that Jack and I haven't been intimate in such a long time Nell…"

"Don't worry, Sharma." Antonella said, in the back of her mind realizing she would not have the opportunity to share her own good news tonight.

Antonella sat Sharma down on the bottom step by the landing, and put her arm around her broad shoulders.

"I felt alone, and trapped, and I needed something." Sharma said, and then positioned her head between Antonella's chin and chest, until she was snug.

"Everyone feels that way from time to time Sharma. Please don't worry."

Sharma moved her head up on Antonella's bony shoulder.

"I sold the property," she said, and started to cry more.

Antonella wasn't surprised, and her fight against the trash plant seemed less important while she consoled Sharma.

After a few minutes, Sharma settled down and told Antonella that what bothered her most was the way she did it.

"I don't know what came over me, I slept with the man who represented the trash plant," she confided.

"We all make mistakes Sharma, don't worry."

"I feel evil. Like I shook hands with Lucifer himself," Sharma cried, gasping for her breath.

"You're not evil Sharma. Don't worry." Antonella knew Sharma was sincere, by the listlessness in her body. "May God, take all her anxiety away," she prayed in her mind.

Then Sharma explained that she didn't cheat on Jack just once, but several times.

Antonella listened, and then said, “Sharma, have pity on him. This man probably does that hundreds of times.” But as soon as she said this, even though she believed it, she realized it might have insulted Sharma. “I mean, not hundreds…”

“That’s alright Nell,” Sharma said, “I know what you mean.”

“No one will know,” Antonella said, and tightened her grip around her.

Sharma sighed, “I wasn’t discreet. Several people were in the bar the night I left with him. It’s a small town. Everyone will know Nell.”

“What was his name?” Antonella asked, and again stumbled to retract her words, realizing her inquiry was pointless, “I mean…”

“His name’s Ryan. Ryan Walsh.” Sharma replied instantly, so Antonella wouldn’t feel embarrassed.

* * *

Immediately Antonella recalled the day her brother Bobby died. There was a knock on the door from Pastor Cirillo, and he embraced her. She recalled the day her mother died at the Hospice in Branford. Her mother held Antonella’s hand and squeezed tight. And Antonella recalled her fifth birthday, and how she found a picture of a man she thought was her father, hidden at the bottom of a shoebox. Her mother told her the man wasn't him, took the picture away, and then hugged her. Antonella sobbed each time.

* * *

Antonella turned and held Sharma by the shoulders, "What is his name?"

"Ryan Walsh," she repeated.

Sharma could tell Antonella was troubled. Her face turned red, and her eyes moistened.

"What's the matter Nell?" Sharma asked, worried for Antonella; but, at the same time, she intuitively knew why Antonella was hurting.

Antonella hugged her again with even more force, "Nothing Sharma, don't worry about anything. We'll get through this. The devil deceives everyone. It's not your fault."

Antonella walked Sharma up the stairs to the widow's walk where they both sat, and had a glass of wine in the darkness.

Sharma thought again about old Mrs. Adams, the crazy women who frequented The Brass Monkey years back, and her tale of a sacred book rumored hidden in the foothills. She recalled what Mrs. Adams had told her about the book, and how its powers protected the people, where it was sheltered, from a weeklong competition of good and evil.

She described the competition as a poker game of sorts for people's souls. It was a story of lust, jealousy, greed and redemption, Mrs. Adams experienced during her youth in Belle Glade, Florida.

She said that during that week, temptations were compressed, like gas in a chamber over a bonfire, so that a reaction was imminent. Mrs. Adams was offered riches to lay with an old state senator. Instead, she married a Mexican gardener, and lived poor. Mrs. Adams chose love: but certain poverty, over riches.

"I guess the book is no longer in the Valley," Sharma mused. "Maybe Mrs. Adams was not crazy at all? Maybe my soul is lost, because I was greedy and chose riches? Maybe I flunked the test and I am damned for all of time?"

* * *

As if Antonella could read the despairing thoughts in Sharma's mind, she spoke in a soft tone.

"Don't let this tear you down, Sharma. We are all flawed souls. For every battle we lose, someone in the world is winning one that can cancel our defeat out… Maybe that person is in Arabia, or Russia, or Israel, or in your bar tonight. But someone, somewhere has our back." She paused.

"We can't let bad things define who we are. Life is all about redemption. You must forgive yourself, Sharma, and we must forgive others."

* * *

After several minutes, Sharma got up, struck a match, and lit the lantern, which hung overhead.

The two friends sat in silence, with Sharma's head resting on Antonella's shoulder. Her blonde hair overlapped Antonella's black waves.

Chapter 24

"I gave all my money away, I gave all my wine away, I gave my daughters away, I gave my shoes away, but I never found truth until I crossed the desert barefooted, and was bite by a serpent." Translated from, The Book of Lost Prophets, *Circa: 1962, A.D.*

Ryan repacked his bags for the trip to Cleveland on Tuesday. Like anyone would be, he was tempted to open Antonella's gift, but he didn't. He left out a suit to wear for dinner; which, in his mind, was a going away party of sorts. Then it dawned on him, why leave?

What did he really have in Ohio? Yeah, he had a good friend in Tony, and a great house; but what did he really have besides that? His job could be done anywhere; all he needed was a computer and a cell phone, so why not stay? Why not see if he and Antonella could make a "go" of it?

"It's funny, but if someone ever told me a week ago I'd be in Derby and not want to leave, I'd say that person was crazy."

Ryan always regarded the Valley, as Death Valley, but now he considered that maybe every day could be as fun and as fulfilling as the past two days.

"Maybe I should stay," he considered.

But at the height of his exuberance, he recalled a cliché his father often repeated, "Truth, like cream, always rises to the top, son."

* * *

Ryan heard that saying just about every day in 1972 during Watergate. Each evening he and his father were glued to the nightly news, and watched the gradual demise of President Richard Nixon.

From the Ellsberg Robbery, to the wiretapping of the Democratic National Committee offices, to John Mitchell, to cashier checks in dubious accounts, to the CIA, to G. Gordan Liddy, to McCord, and Halderman, Ehrilichman, and Kleindienst, and finally to Dean.

They watched as one scandal after another steamrollered, like Godzilla crashing through a Japanese city on his way to destroy some gigantic moth, in the direction of the White House.

The avalanche of events that year, reached a state of critical mass, and created an ideological divide in American politics not witnessed since the Lincoln-Johnson years.

To Ryan, it was the first Reality TV show in history. But bugs weren't being swallowed and weight wasn't being lost, nor amateur singers competing to be crowned the next "idol." A nation tuned in daily, as a Shakespearean type tragedy unfolded before their eyes.

Television sets inside barbershops, inside homes, inside bars, and inside schools were on in epic numbers. Teachers justified rolling out TV's and watched the Senate proceedings, as a civics class, as early as the forth grade.

In all the excitement, Ryan could sense the glee some people took in observing the fall of their nation's leader. Comics loved to coin Nixon's plea, "I'm no crook," and poke fun of him. One comedian, in particular, Rich Little, made a living off of his impersonations of Nixon, by shaking his jowls and throwing his fingers up in the "peace" movement gesture of the times.

"Did truth always rise to the top? Was this why Nixon had to resign, or was he the victim of trusting bad friends? I won't be that trusting of others."

Ryan looked into the mirror. His brown hair needed to be trimmed around the ears, so he jelled it back. He picked up his razor to shave, and determined he could make it work.

"Antonella does not have to find out about me. Sharma will move to the suburbs and no one, besides McHugh, Joe Romanzo, and a few others will know the truth, and they can't speak, because of the money they took."

He slapped on some aftershave, and then reached for his suit coat, resolved to cover up his role in the trash plant.

"The cream won't rise to the top if I don't let it sit. I'll tie up all loose ends."

* * *

It was six o'clock and Ryan decided to drive to Derby and visit a small tavern called Over The Hill. It was a neighborhood bar one street up from Irish Main, and he decided to have a drink before going to Fratelli's to meet Antonella. The Hill was a small bar, which probably fit twenty customers at most, from what Ryan recalled.

In the window was a lighted Schaefer beer sign, and Ryan was amused it was still there as he walked up the seven wooden steps and through the door.

"Oh my God," he thought, "Tugboat Dan."

Ryan sat unnoticed by Dan, who stared into the mirror talking to himself. Ryan could tell he was drunk, but he liked Dan, and he went over to say hello.

When he got closer, he sensed Dan was not happy today. His body odor was a combination of perspiration and alcohol, and his mumblings had the tone of an argument. An issue, he probably worked out countless times, in his head, over a beer. Something most likely caused from his Navy days during the Vietnam War.

Ryan motioned to the bartender to buy them a drink, as he sat on the bar stool next to Dan. Dan turned to Ryan, nodded, then turned back to stare at himself in the mirror, and mumbled to his reflection again. He was smoking a cigar, and kept replaying whatever event he had on his mind, over and over…

Ryan figured it was probably something he didn't get right, and wished he had a chance to try again.

Dan grumbled, turned, and validated Ryan's intuition.

"Ryan, have you ever had a second chance to make something right? To make something bad-good?"

Ryan didn't answer as Tugboat Dan turned back around in his bar stool.

"Before I captained, *The Crack of Dawn*, I owned an auto body shop right after my tour in Nam," he said taking a sip of beer. "It's no secret, Yanz knows," he pointed to the bartender who resembled a stork, "Everyone knows all about it." Dan paused. "I did a shabby job. I cut corners one time and a young boy died."

Ryan's face flushed, when he said this. It sounded too familiar to him. He was quite certain Dan was talking about Antonella's brother Bobby.

"Well, that boy's sister came to my house to see how I was doing the day after he died. Imagine that. I did something that killed her brother, and she's worried about me."

Ryan wasn't sure yet why he was telling him this story.

"Placing blame for accidents is not always clear cut Dan," he said. "Accidents are always messy. I'm sure the death was not your fault."

Dan reached over and grabbed Ryan's left hand. Ryan was startled. Dan's hands were thick and calloused and firm.

"I wanted to help that lady ease her pain. Easing her pain, would ease mine, too," he said squeezing Ryan's hand even tighter. "But today a friend called to tell me my plan failed. It's almost like I killed her brother a second time. That good lady is going to die inside all over again."

Ryan broke free from Dan, and left the bar.

He determined that Dan knew. He figured that Tony's Senator made the calls, and Dan's battleship was scraped.

"Somehow, he knows about me."

Ryan drove past Saint Mary's and considered visiting Father Sheehan, but he was too ashamed.

"He must know, too. Everyone must know," he thought, "How can I face Antonella, if she knows I was behind the trash plant? Maybe she'll understand I was just doing my job. I'm no crook. She'll understand. She'll be hurt, but she'll understand. We connected. I'll go to Fratelli's, and wait for her there. She'll understand."

Ryan felt his cell phone vibrate, then ring. The caller ID showed McHugh's number.

"Yes, McHugh, what do you want?"

"You've been banging Sharma Zawadski?" McHugh yelled into the phone.

Ryan couldn't believe the question. How did he know? Did she tell him? Who else knew? Did Antonella know? Then he realized that all it would take was for one person to see them together, and the whole Valley would know of their affair, because it was such a tight-knit community.

"Pull over ass wipe I'm right behind you," McHugh said.

Ryan looked in his rear view mirror, and saw a white SUV. He pulled over, next to the First Congregational Church, across from the city green, and got out of his car. McHugh pulled in back of him, and met Ryan between the two cars.

"Asshole, I'll have to call a special meeting for Tuesday now to push it through, before P.R.I.D.E. comes out in force. This will hit the papers," he yelled.

Ryan didn't say a word and listened like a child being scolded by his teacher. Just days ago, Ryan had the upper hand on McHugh, now McHugh was in control.

McHugh shook his head, and turned in circles on the heels of his shoes, while tossing insult after insult at Ryan, until he finally crossed the line, and got personal.

"You know what Walsh? You're an asshole just like your father. A loser. You God damn drunk!"

But as soon as McHugh said these words, his whole demeanor changed. His eyes widened and he shut up.

* * *

Ryan called on years of hatred toward McHugh, and his family, and this anger consolidated inside of him. To him the McHughs represented bullying, prejudice, and opportunistic scheming at the expense of the disadvantaged, people not cunning enough to defend themselves.

Ryan visualized what he was about to do. In his youth, he practiced it regularly. Sometimes in front of the bathroom mirror.

He clinched his right hand, and threw a punch straight to McHugh's jaw. As he connected, Ryan heard his jawbone break. At the same time, Ryan felt his own middle knuckle snap, but he felt no pain. McHugh let out a moan, then ducked down to his knees, and sprang up like a boxer. He held up his hands to fight, but Ryan hit him square in the neck, holding back just a little when his fist pressed the bones, and McHugh fell to the sidewalk, gasping for air.

Ryan wasn't done and pulled McHugh up; he pinned him against his white Lexus for one final slug. Then, as he started to follow-through, their eyes met, and Ryan stopped.

The streetlight highlighted McHugh's face, and his pupils stared straight back. But instead of expressing mercy or sorrow, McHugh's eyes seemed to express, "I told you so," and Ryan couldn't hit him.

* * *

Ryan saw himself in a different light, too.

* * *

After all the lessons his father had taught him about forgiveness, and restraint, Ryan realized the same evil that ran through McHugh's veins – ambition, notoriety, greed, lust and self centeredness – ran through Ryan's as well. He was like a brother to McHugh, switched at birth, and given to the wrong parent for raising.

Ryan got in his car and drove back to the hotel. There was no way he could meet Antonella. He needed to get back to Ohio. His role in the trash plant was exposed.

Chapter 25

"Self abandonment is the only true answer." As translated from, The Book of Lost Prophets*, Circa: 1675, A.D.*

At six o'clock on Monday morning, Ryan made arrangements to leave his rental car at the hotel. He took a taxi to Bridgeport, and then caught the 6:30 train to Grand Central, bypassing a departure from Derby. His finger throbbed and was swollen from punching McHugh; he wrapped white medical tape around a Popsicle stick that he found in a wastebasket, and the procedure seemed to help.

For the last three days, he had hoped his stay in the Valley would turn out differently; but now, he knew it wouldn't. He wished he could find a way to resolve some of the childhood issues he felt, but that wasn't to be. He expected to change his bad habits, find a woman like Antonella, and start a new pattern in his life, but he realized that wasn't to happen either.

If he were a betting man, Ryan would not put money on himself. Now, he knew he had to dig down within, and find the strength to live a life he found less and less fulfilling. Today, he only hoped to get by.

He arrived at the Bridgeport station tired and groggy from drinking a half bottle of Dewar's, lamenting about his situation. All night long, he anticipated a knock at the door, but there was none.

First, he expected the police to visit for what he did to McHugh, then he figured McHugh would send some thugs to beat him senseless, next he thought Sharma would come, if for nothing else, to gloat about screwing over a "suit," as she called business people.

Silently, he sat in his room, wishing to get a call from Antonella; but neither his room phone nor his cell phone rang.

The Metro North train that morning was filled with people talking about a pending transit strike on Christmas Eve, but Ryan paid little attention. He was paranoid about the trash plant, and he imagined perfect strangers were whispering gossip about his roll.

Then Ryan's drunk and sick mind revolted. It had had enough, and it made his journey to Grand Central grueling. When Ryan turned to look out the window, the mere reflection of his image off the glass, made him wince. It sickened him.

His head started to spin and he envisioned people he had had an affect on in his life, sitting in the train. Deidre sat by the exit door, with a hollow trance like expression. Seated across from her was a young man with a head wound. He was weeping. Standing in the aisle, he saw dozens of women he had known, all dressed in black negligees.

All at once, the women turned and blew kisses to him. Off at a distance, he heard the far away howls of dogs or wolves, and his head spun faster, like the time he was lost in Grand Central as a young boy.

As if he had fallen through a time tunnel, Ryan was transported to a new cancer ward built at the Griffin Hospital in Derby. There he witnessed the care of young children with kerchiefs on their heads. Three religious men blessed them.

The train darkened, as it went through an overpass, and Ryan sat up and screamed, "No!"

Then, when the train lightened, Ryan was embarrassed to find several commuters staring at him with fearful expressions, and he turned his head away.

"God help me." he thought, "I wish I had never been born." To Ryan, his life was detestable.

But as soon as these cries from desperation surfaced, Ryan took them back.

"Why be a hypocrite? Why cry for His help? I must be brave. It is what it is…"

To make his situation worse, when the train went past Captain's Cove, he saw the USS *Constitution* anchored in the Sound with Dan's tugboat, *The Crack of Dawn*, at its bow. Ryan had crushed his dream, as well as Antonella's and Father Sheehan's. Ryan felt evil.

"It is what it is," he repeated to himself.

When the train arrived in Grand Central, Ryan decided to have a drink at the bar. Ironically, he saw the same odd twin brothers, from the Marriott hotel lounge, seated at a table playing cards, but they didn't notice him. His mind wandered. Were they two brothers on a vacation? Where were they from? Where were they going? Still frightened from the train ride, Ryan imagined their very nature.

"Maybe one is good, and the other evil? Maybe they have been observing my every move like a gambler at a horse track? But which is which?" Ryan decided to move out of their view, and sat behind an ornate support column.

He ordered a Scotch, and hoped the alcohol would pop some life into him and clear his head. And the drink seemed to work. Out of eyesight, he calmly sat at the bar, and checked his boarding tickets out of LaGuardia. Last night, before he drank himself to oblivion, Ryan cancelled his flight out of Newark, and paid for a one-way ticket to Cleveland from Queens. He didn't want the hassle of going to Newark, plus there was an earlier flight out of LaGuardia.

Ryan surveyed Grand Central then remembered what Sharma had told him was located on the Northwest Passage area ceiling. This was the area, which inspired Sharma to have her breast tattooed. Sure enough, he saw the black tiles she mentioned.

"Maybe she is right? Maybe people from the Valley will have my initials tattooed on their chests? Maybe when Jackie Onassis headed the renovation project, she left those tiles black for me and Sharma? Who knows?"

The connection he made between Sharma, Jackie Onassis, and himself, got him to contemplate more. He knew the people in the Valley would not go out and have tattoos with his initials on them, but wouldn't his name be forever associated with the trash plant? If health issues did arise, wouldn't he be somehow responsible for them?

Ryan decided to open up his carry on bag and do some paper work, but in order to grab the folder he wanted, he had to first move the gift Antonella had given him. Ryan was nervous. He knew if he opened the gift, it would probably make him feel even guiltier, but he couldn't resist.

The present seemed to have mega powers; and like a giant magnet from a Saturday morning cartoon pulled a villain to its U shaped poles, against his will, he took the gift out.

Underneath the gold bow and red wrapping paper, was a white box. His hands shook as he pushed aside the tissue, took the gift out, and placed it on the granite bar top. Tears ran down his face.

Here was the answer to a question he never asked. Before him was a ten inch souvenir of the Statue of Liberty. Antonella was the little girl, with the black hair, he had never forgotten since childhood. When a young boy peed in his pants, she was the one who comforted him from the embarrassment, by taking his hand and leading him all the way home to safety.

Now Ryan cried uncontrollably. The bartender came over to ask what was wrong, but he couldn't reply. The man called Security, and two men inquired if there was a problem. They needed to make sure he wasn't having a breakdown, or was a threat to the safety of other people. Ryan composed himself long enough for their satisfaction, and they left.

"How could I abandon her? How could I be so selfish?"

Ryan's arms felt numb and a pain rushed to his shoulder, but he wasn't alarmed, he had felt it before and it always passed. Besides, he didn't care if he had a heart attack and died. Right now, he wanted only to think.

"I am like the Troll Beneath," he mumbled.

Antonella gave Ryan simple things like laughter, and arrowheads, and klings. Mostly, she gave him friendship, asking nothing in return.

Ryan contemplated the time in church, and what Father Cantalamessa had said, "Sooner or later you have to say enough."

Didn't his father basically give the same message when he died? When he said to Ryan, "Soon we all must say enough," wasn't he saying the same thing? It came to Ryan; his father wasn't saying those words excepting death. No, he was saying those words to Ryan expressing life.

A clear vision entered Ryan's mind.

He determined that he couldn't separate sins against his neighbors, and sins against God. To Ryan it was all intertwined. Yes, he knew mistakes were always going to be made, and evil was always going to happen, but Ryan understood he couldn't expect perfection in himself or others. He could no longer let the immobilizing guilt that sin creates define who he was. Like the Troll Beneath, Ryan had to make a decision in his life that was out of his comfort zone.

"Sin is a human condition just like the common cold," he concluded, "and just like a cold, I must take the correct steps to fight it, and get better."

Ryan looked at the Statue of Liberty gift, and he knew what he had to do.

"Sooner or later I Do have to say Enough," he thought. "I have to try to honor God, and fight to do the right thing."

Ryan remembered how he was always too scared to climb and leap, into the water below, from the tenth level at Indian Well. Every time he jumped, it was from level seven. Ryan felt cowardly for never jumping from level ten. He always made excuses for himself. Now Ryan was ready to leap.

* * *

Ryan took the next train back to Bridgeport, and he walked to Captain's Cove Marina to see Tugboat Dan.

"Dan, we need to talk," he said.

Dan was giving the ten sailors, who manned the USS *Constitution*, directions to a local yacht club, the Miamogue, where they could unwind before leaving in the morning for the Merchant Marine Academy in New York.

"Okay, I'm listening," Dan answered.

* * *

By the time they sailed past the section of the river where Sikorsky Aircraft was located, the Coast Guard followed, and Blackhawk helicopters were dispatched to survey the situation.

By the time they saw O'Sullivan's Island approaching in Derby, the river banks were shoulder to shoulder with citizens watching in awe.

By the time Tugboat Dan released the cables, and steered left, to let Ryan and the USS *Constitution* come to a safe and slow stop, news satellite trucks, from Connecticut and New York, were set up and filming the entire crime.

The images of them were viewed worldwide.

ESPN, the sports network, made the short trip from Bristol, Connecticut, and treated it like a championship event. Tugboat Dan and Ryan were members of the Pirates, while their opponents, the Coast Guard, Air Force Reserves, and the FBI, were referred to as the Federalists.

* * *

Now a dream filled Ryan's eye.

* * *

He remembered how his father delighted in the fact that Uncle Louis, his Aunt Mary's husband, was a descendant of Isaac Hull, and Ryan knew his father would be proud of him.

In his minds eye, Ryan pictured his father on the ship, with his arm around his shoulder, smoking an Old Gold, and smiling.

And while they coasted into shore and awaited the Federal Authorities, they listened to the engaging sound of Herb Albert's, "The Lonely Bull," playing in the background.

"I love you," Ryan said.

"I love you," his father replied, and kissed Ryan on the cheek. "Keep us in your dreams and in your prayers, son, until you find your way home."

Then a gust of wind came, and he was gone.

* * *

Meanwhile, the law enforcement officers could do nothing, for fear the USS *Constitution*, which is a living breathing piece of American history, would be damaged. They could only wait, and then arrest Ryan and Tugboat Dan for breaking the law.

Before the authorities boarded and handcuffed Ryan, he spotted Sharma, Antonella and Father Sheehan standing on the island. Then, shouting to get their attention, he put the contract Sharma had signed, above his head, ripped it to small pieces, then threw it into the air like confetti. After all, today was now a festive occasion. The Underdogs had won. A battleship was docked in Derby.

When Ryan was led to shore, one by one the townspeople applauded him and Tugboat Dan for what they had done. Mrs. Duffy approached him and whispered in his ear, "You're an answer to my prayers."

Then, standing before the police car, were Father Sheehan, Sharma Zawadski, and Antonella.

One by one, they came over and gave Ryan a hug. Father Sheehan reached into his pocket, and pulled out his keys. Attached to them was a prayer ring. He pulled it through the loop, and put it in Ryan's front shirt pocket.

"Shalom, Ryan."

"Shalom, Father."

Ryan looked at them smiling.

"Thank you," he said.

Then he looked upwards.

"Th-th-thank you," he whispered and winked.

* * *

The sun shone when Ryan was gifted with truths about his own special life.

* * *

He knew unquestionably that his father was indeed a Nabi-a Prophet, but he came to the conclusion that everyone was a Prophet, too. For good or for bad.

Prophets lost in their own insecurities, and bad habits, given to them at birth and which, if not overcome, held them back from reaching their true potential. Prophets strung together like beads, who God touches to communicate his love, like one bead bouncing against another, which touches another, and then another, and another…

Prophets who need other Prophets to complete themselves, and who must extend a helping hand, to lead each other out of the chaos of a dark and busy world. A world filled with illusions, designed to keep them from living in truth.

As the police car drove off, Ryan turned his head to see Antonella, Sharma, and Father Sheehan standing side by side, with the USS *Constitution* to their backs. Handcuffed, Ryan could only smile; but, one by one, they started to wave.

When they drove past Mount Saint Peter's Cemetery, where his mother and father were laid to rest, Ryan dreamed again about his father, and his inheritance, *The Book of Lost Prophets*.

A hunger grew inside him, that maybe, someday, he could still find that sacred possession in honor of him. And not just for his father; but in honor of all the Prophets who participate in the Word, from every race and religious belief, since the day God breathed an invitation into them to visit his home. Hand in hand in hand.

One small yellow hand wrapped around a large white one, a soft black hand clasped around a calloused red one...

A mystical union with one quest – to get home together.

In his search to locate the lost manuscript, Ryan decided he would start to write his own book. Ryan would visit various cities, and write down words of wisdom from each Prophet he met, and pass them on, then go to the next city, write some more, and pass them on…

"Maybe Antonella will travel with me like she offered the other day at Indian Well," he imagined, "who's to know?"

And when he did write such a book, the first entry would be dated April 5th 1975, which was the day his father passed on his last tidbit of wisdom to him. Ryan envisioned the passage would read: "*Soon we all must say enough.*" Bill Walsh, *The Book of Lost Prophets*, Volume II, April 5th 1975 A.D.

His entire adult life Ryan was haunted by those six words, but now he ran and embraced their meaning.

"There is a fine line between running from something, and running to something," his father once said, "Remember, to those that much is given, much is expected..."

Life never ends…

"A lantern must be in plain view, to be a lantern."

My grandfather is no lie,
The definition of a Great guy!
He's warm and charming,
Funny and Caring,
Who just wouldn't go a mile without sharing.
Even when he's sick and weak
He still shows a light that no one can reach.
While looking into his eyes, I see this man,
Holding so much wisdom and knowledge, It's hard to understand,
I'd like to make it known Pop, that I'm your biggest fan.
He's the grandfather of 24 people, I'm sure God will keep him at the top of his Holy Steeple.
Sure he loves to smoke his cigarettes,
But that doesn't mean you should think of him any less.
He's a good hearted man with a Great wife,
I think he knows he lived an incredible life,
This man is my Grandfather, and I love him a whole lot,
His name is William Joseph,
But better known as Pop-Pop.